Other books by
GABRIEL LANDOWSKI

Miniature Gaming Vol. I
http://www.lulu.com/content/678534

Sons of Dragons
Book 1

The Road of Kyle

Written by

GABRIEL LANDOWSKI

http://www.landowski.info

2007-08

ISBN 978-0-6152-0949-4

Dedicated To

Orson Scott Card

Ender's Game

&

Speaker For the Dead

Joe Haldeman

The Forever War

John Scalzi

Old Man's War

David Drake & S.M. Stirling

The General

"Give a man a fish and he will eat for a day.
Teach him how to fish,
and he will sit in a boat and drink beer all day."

Acknowledgements & Special Thanks

Mary Landowski (my wife)

For your patience, support, encouragement, and love; we made a great cover together! Thank you, my angel.

Nancy Saffioti ('mom')

For your valuable feedback and assistance with editing the grammatical mess I handed you.

Stephen Gates (a mentor)

For showing me that Creativity is not dead and introducing me to the means for sharing it.

Tom Schreiber (a friend)

For being an independent artist and your insight.

CHAPTER I

Private Kyle Evans had to wait for troopers to stow their gear before he could attempt to squeeze by. To load an infantry platoon onto a drop ship took time and the men were not in much of a hurry to be crammed in like sardines. One thing Kyle knew was the officers needed to take their time and load the men and equipment efficiently or there would not be enough room for everything.

Kyle shuffled down the narrow aisle past some more troopers, dropped a carry bag onto his assigned seat, and popped open the stowage compartment door. The space was slightly smaller than the combat pack it was designed to hold and it took Kyle three tries to force the bundle inside.

Another annoyance was trying to slide into the narrow restraint seat with the bulky pockets of his web gear loaded with projectiles and other items of necessity. Platoon Sergeant Rollins had ordered that troopers store their pack loads for the descent to the surface but everyone had to wear their combat vests on the way down. It seemed kind of silly to Kyle as the platoon was to deploy to a relatively passive urban environment where it was to act as a reserve for a military police force. There was no known enemy activity except for a string of protests, which amounted to nothing more than people yelling slogans through amplifiers and waving opposition banners.

Then again there was the old adage to 'train as you fight' but Kyle thought this was taking it a little to the extreme.

In his left breast pocket Kyle felt a copy of '*The Killer Angels*' pressed against his chest as he shifted. He kept it inside the cover of a Bible and snuck it past the sergeants for reading during slow times while off duty. The use of the cover was as close as he was going to get to religion as he decided a long time ago that a belief in Mother Nature and Fate carried more weight with him than the vision of an almighty patriarch. He had been raised to do what he thought was right and help others whenever he could.

I mean, shouldn't that be enough? Besides, doesn't it make me more saintly if I don't expect the reward of an afterlife for all the good I do with mine?

Other troopers continued to shuffle by with their cumbersome loads and equipment swung over hunched shoulders. Kyle waited for the guys from the fourth squad to ease through before he squirmed to better adjust in the restraint seat. Although the combat armor he wore was clipped to him securely, Kyle tightened all the straps even more to make sure there was no trace of slack to be found.

This accomplished, he checked for secure closure on all the various clips to his combat vest worn over the armor. If the flying crate inside of which the troopers had been packed happened to make a rough landing, and they were forced to bail out, Kyle was not going to leave anything loose to get snagged. Two primary ways of dying were always unpopular with him: first to be drowned, and second to be burnt alive. Kyle offered up the suggestion to Fate that he would not like to experience either.

The air in the compartment was cold and crisp, which reminded Kyle of the hospital where he had received his medical checkup. It had a dry, purified quality that made a throat itch. He glanced up at the ceiling where long rows of ventilation inlets poured a fine mist down on the occupants. He briefly wondered what the weather was like on the planet to which they were about to make their Fold.

Kyle inspected the locked carbine in the holster to the left of his seat. The slot both protected the weapon and prevented it from bouncing dangerously around the cabin. Kyle cleared the weapon again for the hundredth time and made sure that no projectile had somehow magically appeared in the chamber. He recalled all the horror stories they were told as trainees about troopers who shot their buddy in the head with an 'unloaded' weapon. That was now a third way that he did not want to die.

Their issued carbines were brand new and Kyle admired his lovingly a he ran a finger over the stamped serial number. The shorter barrel and reduced weight of the weapon was a welcome improvement over the older and heavier training rifles from Basic. It occurred to Kyle that the platoon must be headed toward something real if they had been issued such new equipment.

They give you all this stuff for free and then you suddenly find yourself killing or being killed. It kind of bastardizes the idea of gift giving.

Rested against the seat, Kyle tugged down on the shoulder restraints that would hold him in place. Rollins would make spot checks soon, and if the man discovered the straps were not painfully tight he would immediately initiate 'corrective action'.

First, the towering man would plant his foot next to the shoulder of the offender in order to achieve optimal leverage. Next, he would grip the strap with both hands and apply substantial force to attain a 'sufficient hold' on the trooper. During training several men were reduced to tears and in one instance a guy passed out from the stress of the experience. He realized there was nothing more he could do, so Kyle placed his helmet on his lap and waited for the others to finish the load.

For almost an hour the platoon sat locked in place, slowly losing a battle of wills with the restraints that dug relentlessly into collar bones, shoulders, and necks. Kyle thought of several ways the military could have made the whole experience more tolerable. Unfortunately, the Machine either never had the same thoughts or simply disregarded them. Somewhere on the other side of the compartment a trooper cried out in agony as a squad leader heaved with all his might. The others grinned and chuckled at the pitiful cries of the abused.

I don't know what they're grinning about, any one of them could be next!

None too soon, an announcement began the safety briefing and the fifteen minute countdown to Fold commenced. The

Rosalie, a midget carrier in which they were loaded, would soon perform a wonder of science and disappear from space to emerge in another galaxy many light years from where they had started. The whole process was instantaneous, but the thought of traveling the fabric of the cosmos stabbed him with slight apprehension.

Kyle could not turn his head any reasonable distance to either side while in the seat brace. The idea was to prevent the helmet and neck from whipping around during evasive action or high friction reentry. The immediate effect was to help smother the occupant with a sense of immobilized claustrophobia. Somewhere off to the left Rollins could be heard talking. A cry of pain and anguish sang out and had the desired effect as every trooper still to be inspected tightened his straps yet again. The troopers gritted their teeth under this new level of self-inflicted torture as beads of sweat formed on their brows.

When Rollins did come into view Kyle noted their new team leader in tow. The look of focused attention made it clear that Corporal Rey was dedicated to mastering his new trade. Kyle studied his face and wondered where the soldier was from or what it was that made him volunteer for military service. From what was known of him, most troopers thought he was okay compared to the other corporals, if a bit of a nerd.

How long will it to convert this guy into a professional tormentor like the rest?

The duo finally arrived at the trooper seated to the left of Kyle and everyone in the vicinity fell silent. The natural tendency was to drop the head, almost as if in prayer - which may or may not have been answered. With the blown air overhead Kyle strained to hear the muffled conversation that took place, but made no effort to make eye contact. This was to be avoided at all cost as sergeants and corporals would tend to feel the need to 'train' troopers who eyeballed them. Worse case scenario was the junior leadership who knew you by face and/or name. Then you were automatically volunteered for every detail that needed to be done. Kyle had already lived his own personal hell of continuous Charge of Quarters and Dumpster Duty during Basic.

To his great relief, Rollins simply passed by with Rey in tow. Rollins talked about the effects of loose straps on the human spine and thumped a heavy fist against the shoulder plate of Trooper Chen to the right of Kyle. The soldier only grimaced, with a barely audible grunt. The sergeant then made a point to check for give on the body armor as Rey watched intently. Kyle felt slightly irritated at the man-handling, but some trainers felt that the hands on approach helped a trooper to learn better. Kyle figured it was just an excuse for the instructors and junior leaders to act like sadistic bastards.

When the countdown reached five minutes, the Load Master plugged into the announcement system at the head of the troop bay and officially conducted the Pre-Fold checklist.

"Fiiiive min-ets!"

As per training the troopers echoed the words in a loud and thunderous voice to ensure that all were alert and paying attention.

"FIVE MINUTES! FIVE MINUTES! FIIIIVE MIN-ETS!!"

It was a simple, fast, and effective way to get everyone on the same page and ready to go. If at anytime a trooper had or saw a problem he would shout out a 'no go' command and sergeants would crawl over the problem in a matter of seconds to resolve the issue.

"Ensure restraining straps are tight and secure!"

The imprisoned troopers replied in a unified roar.

"ENSURE RESTRAINING STRAPS ARE TIGHT AND SECURE!!"

All the men heaved senselessly at the straps which had cut into them for the past hour. Fortunately there were no issues thanks to the tedious pre-inspection conducted by the junior leadership. Someone joked about messing with the Load Master, but an senior technician who stood nearby told the offender to knock it off.

"Check your assigned equipment!"

"CHECK YOUR ASSIGNED EQUIPMENT!!"

The troopers reached over feebly to tug at their carbines, or special gear around them, to confirm that it would not come free. Kyle reached over with his right arm, barely able to reach his weapon, which did not budge in the slightest.

"Sound off with equipment check!"

From the back of the troop bay the last trooper in line sounded off with his number and slapped the arm rest of the trooper next in line toward the front.

"Fifteen Okay!"

"Fourteen Okay!"

The process continued until Chen sounded off and slapped the right arm rest next to Kyle who also called out.

"Eight Okay!"

He then slapped the arm rest of Buster to his left and the countdown continued until it reached the squad leader. At this point the squad leader sounded off, slapped his own opposite arm rest, and pointed a flat hand at the Load Master as a visual signal while yelling,

"All Okay Load Master!"

When all of the squad leaders had their hands held out, the Load Master quickly walked past and slapped them in a high five. With the ritual complete and no issues discovered, the Load Master stepped out of the compartment and the drop ship door was sealed. Moments later, the white light of the bay was switched to neon green at either end of the compartment. The troopers were now inspected and ready to roll. Kyle sat watching the mist of the air system, as it continued to descend from the vents. It had taken on the green glow of the compartment making for a surreal experience.

It's just like Yule - well, sort of.

Minutes later the announcement system blared into the compartment as the green lights switched to a warm yellow.

"Thirty seconds!"

"THIRTY SECONDS!!"

Kyle could feel his heart as it began to race and he tried to relax. He quietly reassured himself that he had finished Advanced Individual Training as well as Fold School. He had completed the mandatory five Folds necessary to earn his

Military Occupational Specialty designation. What made him uneasy was a disturbing rumor that the platoon had never completed a single one.

The training classes stated that personnel could not feel a Fold as it occurred. Kyle was convinced that the process somehow irritated the fillings in his teeth, but others insisted that any such notion was purely mental suggestion. One guy claimed the rumor was true, and that the government had faked the training Folds to save on resources and money. Despite this, Kyle and a few others quietly congregated to compare notes on their corporeal experiences.

"T-minus Ten... Nine... Eight... Seven... Six... Five... Four... Three... Two... One..."

For one moment the *Rosalie* held a stationary position in orbit near the Forward Operating Base over the planet of *New Rochelle*.

"...Fold!"

In the blink of an eye the ship winked out of existence, and left only the glittering stars behind. Thousands of light years away in the orbit of another planet there was empty space. A brief flux and the midget carrier appeared with maneuvering thrusters springing to life.

Deep inside the bowels of the ship Kyle felt his teeth tingle, and he mentally cursed the naysayers. A light pressure pushed him to toward the front of the craft. He knew the troopers were loaded on the carrier with the drop ships facing aft. The acceleration lasted for almost a minute before it eased away. The roll of the carrier ceased as well which initiated the state of weightlessness. The trooper across from Kyle spat out a small bubble of saliva from his mouth and everyone watched it tumble away in zero gravity.

There was a brief announcement of a successful Fold and the yellow lights switched back to green. A moment later there was a loud 'thunk' from the hull behind his head followed by a slight shudder. The air flow above him continued to blow, but the rate was greatly reduced. The knowledge that the drop ships were leaving the carrier filled Kyle with a mixture of apprehension and excitement.

Here we go!

* * *

On the bridge of the CVIS *Rosalie,* Commander Michael Milligan listened to the cross chatter of the bridge crew while reviewing a data pad held on his lap. The Fold had been uneventful and without any equipment failure or complication. Major Ayers led the drop ships toward the entry window of the planet and the last of the craft came into view off the port side. While everything ran smoothly, it was just a matter of time before his second in command appeared at his shoulder.

"Captain?"

Milligan smiled slightly to himself.

"What you got Pete?"

Lieutenant Commander Peter Freedman lowered his voice slightly and leaned in closer.

"Sir, we have not been able to locate the approach beacons for *Watkins 6.* We've rerun the possible encoded signal queries but received no beacon responses. It appears that they are not functioning – or are not there at all."

Milligan found this of interest, and pondered the possibility that the Flight Control Station over the planet had purposely switched off the beacons. He turned back to Freedman.

"So we don't have anything at all?"

His number two gave a short shake of his head.

"Not a thing. We've run an immediate diagnostic and system self-check which came back okay, so we aren't experiencing a mechanical issue on our end. The communications spectrum is completely blank, and the surface shows no sign of traffic. The only thing we're getting is the normal radio activity from the planet core and space."

Milligan put down the data pad and sat back in his command chair to consider the situation. The Flight Controller might have turned off the beacons, but there was no way to make the whole planet silent. With a population as large as the one on *Watkins 6* it was impossible to eliminate all the communications traffic that could be emitted.

Unless there had been some sort of attack.

Milligan turned to Freedman.

"Any sign of hostile action?"

Freedman's brow furrowed as he shook his head.

"As best we can tell, sensors picked up a scattering of debris circling the planet. It could have come from a small installation, but there are no obvious signs of attack. The alarming thing is the planet itself. It seems devoid of any cities, ports, or technology."

Milligan sat up at this.

"None?"

Freedman shook his head.

"None at all, sir. Navigation is checking the calculations, but Lieutenant Green believes that this may not be *Watkins 6*. Right now we're running a confirmation using the Star Field Positioning system."

Milligan cocked an eyebrow.

"Green doesn't think this is *Watkins 6*? Then where in the hell did he Fold us to?"

Freedman only shrugged his shoulders slightly and looked perplexed.

Milligan turned back to the view of the planet and realized for the first time that he had no idea which one it was. The sphere shared many similar characteristics of the life-supporting worlds the Fleet visited, but the more he stared at it the less familiar it became.

Damn.

"Better reign in the infantry then and circle the drop ships back until we can figure this out. Tell Green I want to know where he took my ship and I want to know now!"

Freedman gave a short nod and floated past the bridge crew giving hushed commands. Green looked up with apprehension from where he stood over his technicians who furiously worked the computers.

Milligan had spent eighteen years in Fleet but had never been in a situation like this before. In all his time at the Academy there had been some theoretical vignettes which involved a breakdown of the Fold process, but they were mostly exercises to build confidence. With his nerves already set on edge, the burden of command caused a burning sensation in his stomach.

What have we gotten ourselves into?

* * *

Kyle closed his eyes, slumped in the seat, and tried to fall asleep to make time pass more quickly. The troopers had trained to remain strapped in place for upwards of four torturous hours but most landings took less than two. In training they had even undergone an endurance simulation for an insane eight straight hours while a computer faked a whole series of accidents and mishaps. Troopers puked or pissed themselves and then were forced to sit in their own emissions until the sequence terminated. At the end, the cadre opened the waist doors to the training facility and unmercifully hosed them down with ice water.

There was a sudden loud curse from up front. Kyle opened his eyes and heard Master Sergeant Holly as he conversed with the crew of the drop ship. Kyle strained to lean forward and could see the heads of the squad leaders looking to each other and then back to the platoon sergeant. Holly gave a curt acknowledgement before he swung the boom microphone away from his mouth and shook his head.

Kyle asked the second squad guys who were positioned closer to the sergeants,

"What's going on?"

They, too, tried to read lips or strained to hear over the rush of air from above.

"Not sure - looks like we're turning around and heading back."

Kyle looked at the faces of the troopers across from him and slumped back into the restraint seat to ponder.

What in the hell can we be going back for?

Another idea crossed his mind and Kyle fumed bitterly to himself.

This had better not be another fucking rehearsal!

As the idea became a possibility Kyle felt the drop ship tip up as it executed a turn.

Fuck the army.

* * *

Peter Freedman felt uncomfortable as he reappeared at the elbow of his captain.

"Sir?"

Milligan nodded his head for Freedman to continue.

"Sir, we have a problem. We're definitely not over *Watkins 6.*"

At this Milligan looked up with anger and controlled his alarm.

I'll space that bastard Green!

"What the hell do you mean 'we're not'!?"

Freedman appeared to struggle under Milligan's fierce glare.

"We don't know how it happened, but the Fold placed us at the wrong location in space. I double checked Lieutenant Green's plots and the sequence logs to ensure the execution was correct. Somehow during the Fold our destination concentration was shifted and we ended up here."

Milligan remained silent taking it all in. Freedman continued,

"We're running a star match now and trying to determine exactly where we are, but so far initial stored searches are coming up negative. Positioning is running a series of theoretical plots to see if the computer can extrapolate where we are, but as of right now it appears to be uncharted space."

Milligan was dumbstruck.

Uncharted space is nothing new with these drives but how did the Fold miss its mark? More importantly, the question is whether we can make a Fold back. I don't like this – I don't like it at all.

Milligan knew that in the past when Fold technology was first pioneered there were a number of test ships that never returned for reasons unknown. Over the next century research had perfected the technology into an art form. Nevertheless, there had been situations where ships came out of Fold a few hundred meters from their mark. Nothing in known history had ever redirected the concentration of a Fold, especially that of a ship the size of a midget carrier.

Milligan felt a cold stab of pain in his chest.

This might be a natural phenomenon but it could be man made. Heaven help us if this is a new enemy capability!

Milligan turned to Freedman and made his best effort to contain his concern, but failed to do so for the most part.

"Secure all drop ships. I want that star match on the double. Tell Watch to keep their eyes peeled. We're dealing with an unknown situation here, and I don't want to be surprised by anything sneaking in under the scopes. Triple check that Navigation did not screw up the Fold. Let me know the instant the plot is checked and the drive passes a complete diagnostic."

Freedman appeared startled as Milligan rattled off the list but quickly recovered and departed. His orders to the bridge had a sense of urgency and a slightly higher volume to which the crew instinctively responded. Milligan began to scan the field of stars before him, and searched for some hint as to what they had stumbled into. The twinkle of lights did not reveal their secret.

What the hell is going on here?

Tense moments ticked by with a number of the drop ships returning to their assigned bays. Milligan could still see the last of the flight on its way back from the planet which hung in the distance. The current speed at which they traveled would bring them home to safety in the next few minutes.

Freedman reappeared and handed Milligan a data display.

"Sir, based on the initial readings there is a huge energy wave fading rapidly which originated approximately at the time of our arrival. I don't know how it was accomplished or what caused it, but it appears that our Fold destination was indeed hijacked…"

"Contact!"

The bridge fell dead silent as the Watch station made the call. Milligan spun around to the officer on duty who furiously adjusted the display screen before her.

"What do you have?"

Her mouth was a thin line of concentration.

"Sir! Contact bearing sero-three-sero mark sero-four-six, range five kilometers. It's a class three signature and unidentified with no transponder. The active scan detected its propulsion burn as it moved to realign on us."

No transponder and masked to sensors except for a propulsion burn signature. Could be a craft coming in blind in order to fool our sensors. For all I know I'm sitting right in the center of a civilian glide path!

Milligan weighed his options and decided on caution and the preservation of his ship. He turned back to Freedman and ordered,

"Secure the ship and sound Battle Stations."

"Aye, aye sir!"

The overhead speakers blared with Freedman's amplified voice,

"This is the Bridge - all hands to Battle Stations, this is not a drill! All hands Battle Stations, this is not a drill!"

The entire bridge scrambled; Milligan turned back to the main view and watched as the last of three drop ships closed the distance toward them. He cursed under his breath.

Damn hot shot pilots always have to make a race out of things! They've managed to string themselves out but good.

He turned back to Freedman and inquired,

"How long until they're inside?"

The second in command looked out the main screen at the small craft as they barreled toward them.

"At least two minutes."

Milligan cursed under his breath again.

I'm not going to expose this ship to danger trying to slip them inside.

To Freedman he ordered in a low tone,

"They're not going to make it inside the protective envelope in time. Tell them to hold off and wait at a safe distance until this is concluded."

Freedman nodded his head and turned to Communications.

"Tell the remaining Zulu elements to hold at heading three-sero-sero mark three-sero-sero, range of two thousand meters, until further ordered. Let them know that we're activating our protective envelope and are at Battle Stations."

The officer nodded his head and pointed to a technician who began to hail the ships.

* * *

Kyle continued to watch the troopers, who in turn watched Master Sergeant Holly grow more irate. Something had to of happened to piss off the seasoned veteran.

Without warning the cabin lights flickered to a harsh red glow. The drop ship rolled to the right and Kyle felt himself pressed against the troop seat. The maneuver was much more aggressive than the previous turn. Somewhere off to his right a trooper complained softly to his buddy but fell quiet as the weaving continued. It dawned on Kyle that this was not a drill.

Something is definitely wrong.

* * *

"Contact! We have a new inbound bogey bearing original contact location and closing fast! Looks like our primary blip launched a drone or missile at us!"

Milligan sat up in his chair and hit the auto lock which secured him to his seat while he shouted,

"Counter measures and defensive fire!"

As he spoke the point defense guns and counter measure launchers on the ship came alive. Flares streaked away from the midget carrier while guns hurled glittering specks into the path of the incoming object. Milligan tried to follow the reach of the guns and the trail of the flares.

Within a moment there was a flash that nearly blinded them.

"Incoming destroyed!"

The defensive guns ceased but the occasional flare continued to launch. Milligan began to speak but was interrupted by another flash – more than one incoming had been aimed their way.

"Counter Measures! Keep that screen up but pace it so you don't bleed us dry! Last thing I want is to give them a fire works show till we're empty and then have them knock us out. Helm, bring the ship to a head on alignment with the contact and keep our profile thin! Navigation, prepare for an emergency Fold on a reverse course plot!"

Freedman stood at his elbow and whispered softly,

"Sir, we still have those remaining drop ships…"

Milligan roared at him.

"I know! I know!"

Freedman visibly flinched then glanced at the crew around him. Milligan struggled to get his emotions in check before he continued in a controlled voice,

"I have no idea who is taking pot shots at my ship. I have no idea how we got out here in the middle of nowhere. For all I know these hostiles hijacked our Fold concentration and pulled us into an ambush. That's never been reported possible before, and Fleet will need to know about it. We're getting the hell out of here and will circle back with reinforcements as soon as we have a better idea about what happened!"

Freedman nodded his head but appeared hesitant before he turned and issued the order.

I know what you're thinking Peter, but you're not sitting in the hot seat. They can put me in front of a Board of Inquiry all they want later on but right now I'm getting my boat to safety!

Lieutenant Green called out from Navigation,

"Sir, we have the reverse plot entered!"

Milligan glanced out the main view as the defensive guns fired and flares launched from his ship. For a long moment he hesitated. A star winked out of existence as if something had passed in front of it which jarred him back to reality.

"On my mark!"

Heaven help me. Heaven help them!

"Fold!"

"Aye!"

A moment later they were gone.

* * *

Everyone in the drop ship paid intense attention to the front of the troop bay. The environment doors had closed between the troopers and the cockpit, and Master Sergeant Holly spoke into his microphone in a gruff and clipped manner. Kyle knew there was only one reason for the doors to be closed, which was confirmed a moment later by the pilot who came on with an announcement.

"We have a hostile contact making a run on the carrier. You boys get ready in case we need to do some flying."

Kyle went cold and tugged at his restraint straps for the hundredth time. He had not loosened them in the slightest since the launch from the *Rosalie*, but training forced him to recheck just in case.

What in the hell is going on here? This was supposed to be a cake walk deployment babysitting a bunch of whining city boys!

Glancing over at his carbine Kyle could see it was still held securely in the rack. He reached up and checked his chin strap and clipped his helmet to the seat headrest. He then hooked his wrists and ankles securely so no part of his body would whip around during the rapid maneuvers that were sure to follow.

Holly came in over the helmet radio on the platoon frequency.

"Listen up! The drop ships can do spins and whirls that would make a rollercoaster look like it's standing still! Unless you want to be scrubbing the insides of this vehicle and all the gear it contains, I strongly urge you to get a barf bag on right now."

Kyle, with his head locked in place, glanced with his eyes toward the sergeants and realized none of the trapped troopers wore the bags. The idea of course was that if a trooper heaved his guts the vomit would go through the one-way valve inside the bag and not spray across the whole cabin. Just thinking about floating globules of chunky barf was enough to make Kyle queasy.

He unhooked his wrist to pull the bag out of a slot in the seat and placed the open end over his mouth. A large elastic loop fit over his helmet and held the contraption snugly against his face. Now, if Kyle puked, the pleasure of the experience and the smell would be his and his alone to enjoy.

One more reason this is the greatest job in the universe!

As he thought about loose stuff flying around the cabin, Kyle also decided to drop his eye protection. He reached up with a quick twist, and the helmet visor dropped down to cover his eyes past his cheekbones. He hooked his arm back into the seat loop as he took another breath to calm himself.

Alright you bitches – do your worst.

He expected the ship to start the spin-and-whirl routine at any moment, but was surprised to hear the engines simply shut down. A second later the cabin went pitch black with an alarmed chorus of muffled voices.

Master Sergeant Holly chastised them,

"Shut the fuck up!"

The startled troopers fell silent.

"Listen up! We are gliding dead to see if we can slip away from the mothers who are trying to kill us. You ladies keep your dresses on and your mouths shut! One word out of you, and I'll space the whole fucking platoon through the air lock!"

The message from the senior man was clear, as reflected by the absence of the usual piss-ant comments from the enlisted men. Kyle and the rest of the troopers sat in bound silence and waited for the engines to kick on, or the blinding flash and depressurization that would signal their demise.

I wonder if it is better to die in the explosion, or from exposure to depressurization.

He carefully imagined what both would be like and decided he did not want to find out. Glancing up he could make out the internal helmet clock and noted the current time. If the platoon was to sweat it out in the darkness Kyle would at least have an idea of the duration.

Not that we want to start setting any new world records...

* * *

The troopers continued to glide 'dead' for almost six hours after the *Rosalie* made the exit Fold. The rogue contact had broken off its attack and headed back out to open space at almost the same instant the midget carrier had disappeared. The drop ship pilot reported to Holly that the unidentified craft executed a Fold of its own, which left the three loads of troopers alone – isolated. Within minutes, the red emergency lights were on again in the troop bay and the men waited silently for the next hand of Fate to be dealt.

After another half hour passed, the troopers began to get restless and soon trips to the head were in demand. The white lights switched on as troopers started a rotation to the cramped closet taking turns to relieve their strained bladders and bowels. The process was made all the more fun by having to maneuver and perform their duty in zero gravity.

Several troopers found it hard to adjust to the altered equilibrium experienced with weightlessness and filled their barf bags with vigor. Others simply sat and talked in low voices or slept like babies. Kyle was still highly energized by the brief encounter and could not figure out how anyone could even think about sleeping.

The hours continued to pass without the return of the *Rosalie* and troopers began to get restless. The flight leader held a brief powwow with the ranking officer aboard one of the other drop ships and the decision was made to go dirt side. Those troopers floating about were pulled ungracefully through the air by buddies and guided to their seats where they strapped in. The previous lengthy inspection was reduced to a cursory check of personnel and equipment. Once the squad leaders were snug in their seats, Master Sergeant Holly updated the pilot and the drop ship began to accelerate.

Within minutes the thrumming of the engines grew into a roar and the craft began to vibrate violently. Kyle knew the drop ship was entering the atmosphere of the planet and that soon they would be on the ground. For what it was worth, the knowledge brought a small sense of relief – if they did not burn up on reentry. Then again, Kyle realized that he had no idea what to expect on the surface anyway.

The drop ships successfully entered the upper atmosphere and the pilots debated a landing zone. Because this planet was not *Watkins* 6, no one had an idea who might be on the surface. A cursory scan revealed no obvious urban areas or ports, only densely packed mountains sprinkled with wooded valleys. The most obvious feature was a large body that appeared to be an ocean but upon closer inspection proved to be a vast steppe. The large grassy plain was devoid of trees and went on for miles in every direction.

Taking into consideration cover and concealment the pilot led the flight into a deep mountain valley where there appeared to be water and sufficient forest. The infantry commander selected a landing zone and the ships all touched down with a jarring thud. Kyle, bathed in sweat, looked skyward and gave silent thanks to whatever divine spirit had brought him back to solid ground in one piece.

Once the troopers freed themselves and their equipment, they disembarked to a hastily formed perimeter. The sergeants yelled, cursed, poked, and prodded the troopers into place. Within moments the confused gaggle managed to expertly fade into the surrounding conifers.

With the infantry off-loaded, the flight leader ordered the drop ships to a hide position within communication range that had both orbital cover and concealment. A large cavern at the head of the mountain stream would serve as a perfect natural hanger.

As the last drop ship powered up and lifted off from the landing zone it blew one last annoying gust of needles and small branches. Kyle twisted onto his side from a position under a pine tree to watch the craft depart. Roaring away low over the tree tops, it disappeared after the others and a silence fell over the valley. Rolling back onto his stomach, Kyle scanned the terrain's natural features, familiarizing himself with his new surroundings.

Any time he tried to get settled in a sergeant shifted him to a new location. After being moved a fifth time it was well into the evening, and Kyle figured he would not be relocated. No sooner had he made himself comfortable, and then he was pulled through the forest to yet another location. By that time it was too dark out to see the terrain in front of him; even the ambient light was insufficient for his low-light visor to be of any use. For all he knew, Kyle was aimed at the rest of the platoon.

This is a hell of a way to fight a war. I don't know how it could get any worse than this!

It began to rain in a steady, penetrating downpour.

Great, just great.

The temperature dropped noticeably and a biting chill began to set in. Reaching into his pack, Kyle freed a thermal blanket and a heavy wet-weather poncho to wrap around his back and shoulders. The ground was covered in a type of long conifer needle which provided a fair amount of insulation below him. The rain increased in intensity and it took no time at all for his exposed legs to be soaked to the bone. Several times Kyle watched his own breath appear as he exhaled, and his hands and feet ached in the harsh conditions.

During the course of the night it became extremely difficult to relax. Even after being relieved from watch Kyle found it difficult to sleep. The time was spent wondering who attacked them and whether or not enemy infantry would be deployed against them. The main question on his mind was why the drop ships had not left them in the city where they were supposed to be.

One rumor had it that the *Rosalie* had been destroyed, but once Holly caught wind of the scuttlebutt he personally made the rounds to eliminate it. He clearly stated that the ship had made an emergency Fold back to *New Rochelle* and was mounting a relief expedition. He also made it clear that any talk to the contrary would result in his boot up the ass of the offender. A veteran of almost three decades, Holly knew the effect on morale and discipline that wild imaginations could cause.

Kyle thought about the ammunition stored in the pouches of his combat vest. His temporary team leader had made the rounds earlier for an equipment check and handed him a full load of projectiles. This was in addition to the initial load he had originally drawn. The weight of the additional ammunition felt weird against his body and he wondered if the sergeants would be passing out the grenades and mines next. He then thought about nervous troopers handling the ordnance in the dark and decided it was a bad idea. The last thing he wanted to do was die from some other idiot getting excited with an explosive device. This became the fourth way he did not want to die.

Kyle loaded a brick of projectiles into his carbine but did not chamber the first round. He was still deathly afraid he might accidentally shoot someone and the unloaded chamber provided another layer of safety. Granted, it also slowed down his reaction time to a potential enemy attack. Nevertheless, at that time, shooting a friendly was more of a possible risk.

The password and counter password were circulated and then changed again an hour later. Someone quipped that the newest combination was 'we're fucked'. Kyle grew angry at the reckless behavior and refused to pass it on.

Dip shits – this isn't a game!

As the night wore on Kyle rotated into and out of his watch with his battle buddy. Sanchez was from a different platoon entirely, as was the squad leader that checked in on them. In the hectic shift of the perimeter he had been easily separated from his team. All Kyle wanted to do was stay dry and in one place. The last thing on his mind was to wander around looking for his buddies.

The pine needle bed remained comfortable with the thermal blanket and poncho keeping his torso warm. With the adrenaline gone and the warmth of his bedding, staying awake was the current challenge. As he started his next hour-long watch, Kyle did his best to shake off the drowsiness as he stared out into the dark forest beyond.

He tried to scare himself into remaining more alert by pretending the worst was about to happen. Kyle silently berated and reminded himself of the importance of doing his job. The enemy could walk up to his position, kill him in his slumber, and then begin to systematically eliminate the rest of the squad.

The woods to his front remained quiet and unchanging; the unsubstantiated fear had done little to get his blood pumping. He knew that he would catch hell if he allowed himself to lapse in a moment of weakness just to catch some shut eye.

Even the threat of an enraged Holly discovering him lacked the expected incentive.

And that guy scares me worse than the enemy!

Minutes later, and despite his best effort, Private Kyle Evans committed the most basic crime a soldier could; he fell fast asleep.

* * *

CHAPTER II

The stag slowly stepped to the edge of the field and raised its antlered head. The morning breeze blew a collage of scents across his snout and he carefully tried to pick out the doe.

Cool air from the foot of the mountain tops flowed over the waving field of grass on the gentle slope. The stag looked about the small clearing and considered the best direction to continue pursuit.

Something drew him to the right and he began to trot softly along the edge of conifer trees. The scent of the doe was strong in the general area and she must have passed that way only a few minutes before.

He continued to breathe in the scent of his desire, and pictured where she was heading. It could be down by the water for a cool drink, or on the opposite side of the field, where younger trees might provide a safe place to rest. All he needed to do was catch up with her.

At the base of a grassy patch the trail turned uphill and the stag followed. As he neared a jutting piece of wood another scent alerted his senses. It was a peculiar odor unlike anything he had ever known before. As he approached a dense thicket of brush he slowed his pace and grew more wary of the smell which he could not place.

Not quite spooked, he halted and stared hard at the dense brush a few lengths off trying to discern motion or shapes. The smell was overpowering and the stag knew that this was definitely something that he had never encountered before. As alarm grew he turned his head to the left and ensured that nothing crept up on him from behind. Instinct directed that he should back away and pursue the doe by the route he had considered earlier.

KPOW!

There was a tremendous blow which smashed the air from his lungs. The blood in his head began to rush with adrenalin. The stag tried to run but his step simply dissolved and he slid to the ground in a heap. For a brief moment he laid there and tried to catch a breath that would not come. The stag could taste blood in its mouth and every fiber of his being screamed for him to run.

But he could not.

After a few moments he heard nothing but his rapid heartbeat; as it began to slow the world faded to an eternal black.

* * *

Kyle felt his heart jump in his chest as the rifle fired. The magnificent stag had come to within twenty meters of their hide position before Corporal Kelly dropped it. The entire experience had been surreal.

The two troopers had spent the predawn darkness creeping out to the edge of the grassy field. As silently as possible, they quickly crawled into their hide position. Kyle recalled from the previous instruction that any excessive noise, movement, or smell could spook their prey.

It had been a month since the emergency landing on the surface and the troopers had remained as vigilant as they possibly could during that time. As the first week passed an expected enemy attack failed to materialize. Subsequently, the priority then became making life more comfortable. Above all, was the constant search for food.

The ranking officer was First Lieutenant Taylor who had ordered a defensive position be established. The troopers set to work digging underground bunkers in which to hide from hostiles and the elements. The next order of business was food and water to sustain them as the combat rations were in short supply. Finding water was easy enough with numerous mountain streams to choose from. The rocky terrain, however, had not lent itself to the growth of edible plants beyond wild onions and a type of dark purple berry. The only remaining alternative was the local game animals.

An initial foraging party had gone out and found a series of small trails no bigger than a foot path. Observation teams were then placed to watch the most likely traveled routes. They discovered the only traveler was a type of small deer with a blotched coat of brown and mossy green. The camouflage helped the animal to blend in with the surrounding terrain and made it nearly invisible when it stood motionless.

With the combat rations reduced to one packet a day the troopers would be starving in less than two weeks. The berry and onion collection produced a good amount of vegetation to eat but no man wanted to live on a stinky fruit salad. The small streams turned up some small fish, and the rocky crags an occasional fowl or eggs, but there was not enough to provide a regular source of protein for so many.

After a brief conversation at headquarters, word was passed for anyone with hunting experience to report to the command post. There, the handful of troopers worked out a plan with Taylor and Holly guaranteed to bag some meat. Thus organized, the four volunteers set out to see what they could produce. The hope was that the little bastards were as tasty as they were cute.

Fortunately, they were.

After two days of selecting a good firing position and figuring out the best way to take the shots, the team settled in and waited for the early morning light to come. As the dawn grew in intensity the troopers easily spied a small herd of the deer grazing near a steep bluff and took four of them in the same moment. The shots sounded as one and echoed back down the valley to the hungry men. A brief radio call from Taylor confirmed that the team had been successful and the troopers were bringing meat within the next four hours.

The team emerged with their fresh kills swinging from portage poles. The meat was brought to the kitchen area and the assigned cooks went about the task of dressing it. A majority of the animal's diet appeared to be the thick stalks of the wild onion.

To stretch the food supply, a large stew was made inside a sterilized container lid; it contained a generous amount of onion and the more recently discovered mushrooms. The result was generally agreed to be gamey in nature and most thought the double dose of onion too much. In the end, starving troopers could not be choosey and the stew was quickly consumed allowing the diners to bitch about the lack of quantity.

With this newfound success each trooper was then ordered to learn and master the art of hunting. Each squad would take turns providing food for the unit and conduct limited patrols in search of good hunting spots. Corporal Kelly was the designated primary instructor who taught Kyle and squad how to bag and tag the little beasties. Having grown up in the outskirts of a major city, hunting and gutting animals were alien concepts to them.

Kelly motioned to Kyle and Buster to retrieve the stag he just shot. The two rushed out from the concealment of the brush at a crouched trot. The troopers scanned the surrounding tree line as they approached the stag and Kyle circled around the non-hoof side of the animal where it lay. He reached down with a stick and touched it to the animal's eye. It did not react. Convinced the animal was dead, the two troopers slung their carbines across their backs and took hold of it by the legs.

It took the two troopers a minute to carry the stag back to the trees as it was much heavier than its small size suggested. As they neared the edge of the brush several others jumped out to help them maneuver the catch further into the woods.

The animal easily weighed over a hundred pounds, and the antlers were miniature but impressive with twelve unflawed points. Kelly looked down at his prize with a large grin on his face and whispered in an excited voice,

"Check that out boys, check that out! He may be tiny but that rack is just a beaut!"

Everyone smiled as they stood around and looked at the deer up close for the first time. The troopers engaged in small talk as Kelly continued an initial inspection of his prize. The corporal then pointed out some characteristics that distinguished males from the females and listed different warning signs which might indicate sickness in the animal. With the preliminaries completed it was time to get down to the business at hand.

"Alright you bad-ass killers, time to get bloody."

Kelly reached into his hip pouch and produced a small folded blade which he then offered to Kyle. It was a little nerve racking to consider the first cut into an animal that had been breathing less then five minutes ago. Kyle looked down at the opened glassy eye of the stag and felt a slight quiver of pity.

Sorry dude. I'll do my best not to waste what you have to offer.

He placed his hand on the chest of the animal and found it still warm to the touch. It reminded Kyle of petting the family dog back home, and he had to push the thought out of his mind.

Alright, enough of that. This isn't a game and you don't have time for bullshit. Just gut the thing and get it over with.

Four other troopers took hold of the legs of the animal as instructed by Kelly. The corporal then explained to Kyle what needed to be done and what needed to be avoided. The others listened in silent anticipation while the security teams sat a little way off scanning for bad guys.

Kyle attempted to make the initial cut; squeamishness changed to annoyance as he found it difficult to pierce the tough hide of the creature. After several attempts Kelly leaned in and pinched a thick wad of the animal between his fingers and gestured to his student.

"Like this Evans, just grab up the skin to lift it off the ribcage and then push the tip of the blade into the sternum. This way if you go too far you hit bone and the internal organs won't empty all over your meat."

Kyle had done as instructed and the knife made easy headway after the tip managed to cut through. Thinking back to medical training in the classroom he expected to see an ocean of blood and gore. Much to his surprise the inside of the animal was very neat and organized. Kyle widened the cut as directed. The experience was more similar to a dissection than anything else. Kelly leaned in again and pointed out several items of interest.

"You'll also see that by taking this guy in the throat area I minimized the internal damage and avoided the guts. I want you to think about having to cut into the animal if I had shot him in the intestines. Remember: aim for the point above the front legs toward the chest of the animal. Never shoot from the front or you'll be digging through ruptured guts and eating shit tainted meat."

A little slice here, another one there. Cut loose this tendon, but don't puncture that sac.

Kyle was half listening when the tip of the blade caught for a moment, only to pop free and sink effortlessly into the knuckle of his hand. Examining his injury and inhaling through pursed lips, Kyle gently bent the finger until a large gash appeared in the skin.

Yep, I got myself good.

Cussing, he withdrew his hand and watched the wound until blood began to flow freely. Kyle let it bleed a second or two which helped to wash out the wound. He glanced up in silent frustration at Kelly who shook his head.

"Shit Evans, you think you'd be able to handle a knife by now, infantry boy. Pop out of there and clean that up before it gets infected. The rest of you, forget anything you might have heard about drinking or eating something raw from a kill to prove how much of a bad ass you are. If the animal has a virus you're taking that straight into your body and you'll likely make yourself sick and die. Don't be cool, be alive."

Reluctantly Kyle handed the small skinning blade to Buster, and then applied pressure to his finger to staunch the flow of blood. He poured disinfectant into the wound which caused it to burn like hell. Afterward Kyle had a little difficulty in opening the protective wrapper and placing the small bandage over the cut. The other troopers continued to watch Buster finish the job that Kyle had started.

A few moves of the blade later and the stomach accidentally burst with a wet popping sound. The smell of onion, decomposing grass, and blood gagged them all. The overpowering odor was similar to a filthy urinal after several weeks of summer heat.

Kelly laughed at them and then quickly demonstrated how to get the stomach contents off the carcass. If the troopers failed to recover the meat correctly all their hard work would be for naught. Kelly dumped out the internals and the men, fighting back the urge to puke, wiped the meat off as best they could. The corporal then picked through the guts and showed which were good eating and how to pack them for transport. With this done Kyle and Buster buried the unusable remains to help hide the smell of the kill.

After much cursing and swearing the squad earned the privilege of carrying the carcass back to the main post. The animal was now lighter but still heavy as hell. After they slipped and slid down the wet clay path for half an hour the exhausted troopers made it back. On arrival they turned their shouldered load over to the kitchen crew.

* * *

Two weeks later Kyle was selected to join the hunting detail for the squad. This time the troopers would be going it alone. Corporal Rey checked their equipment and clothing as the hunting patrol would be out for several nights. After a final communication check with the company Tactical Operations Center, the troopers passed through the defensive perimeter and disappear into the wooded countryside.

Rey led them in a loose column up the stream bed and toward a good hide position that he learned of from a buddy in the other platoon. The patrol approached the release point and Rey called a halt to quietly explain how he wanted to proceed.

"So when we leave the release point, Reeves and Buster will go to the left through the woods and wait at the end of the field. Once Kyle and I get into our hide position, I'll call you guys to start pushing. Make enough noise as you move across our front to drive anything in hiding without panicking it. The idea is for you to kick up and push any deer in front of you to where Kyle and I can get a shot at it."

The two troopers just nodded their heads in response. As they got up to leave Reeves commented casually,

"Just don't pop a round in our heads by accident Corp."

Kyle looked at Rey who just grinned.

"I'll shoot you in the ass just for the fun of it!"

Rey led Kyle forward on all fours as the two tried their best to not be detected. They kept a watchful eye for grouse that might burst into the air and warn everything in the vicinity. The birds were too small for eating but the troopers wanted to kill them anyway for the near heart attack they caused.

The hide spot was located behind a slight rise underneath some tall pines, which provided the hunters concealment and overhead cover as they waited for the prey. Although the weather had turned noticeably cooler, a dense mist kept warm air close to the valley floor. A thick carpet of pine needles underneath them guaranteed welcome protection from the cold ground.

The sniper rifle was pulled from a carry bag and prepared for action. Although the hunters had their carbines along, the rifle had more range and better stopping power. Like the other small arms issued to the common foot soldier it was powered by pressurized air. It, however, utilized a sabot slug which did an excellent job of slapping down a large target. The smaller penetrating projectiles of the carbines had a tendency to pass through the target and carried most of the kinetic energy with them. A regular experience was to hit the animal with a carbine and it would take off and survive most of the time whereas, the slug had a tendency to knock the creature down where it stood. Rare was the animal that took more than a few steps after getting whacked by the soft slug.

Once the rifle was assembled and the power sight adjusted, the two got comfortable and Rey hailed the push team via his helmet microphone.

"SLAUGHTER 1, this is SLAUGHTER 6, OVER."

The right headphone in the helmet Kyle wore was tuned to the squad frequency and echoed Rey as he spoke. Kyle laughed to himself,

Slaughter. It had better not be. If they slaughter anything then they can clean out the entrails!

"SLAUGHTER 1, this is Slaughter 6, OVER."

"SLAUGHTER 6, this is 1 – go ahead, OVER."

"Alright dudes, we're in position. You guys can start walking that far tree line to our front. BREAK."

Rey fragmented his transmission into short messages to make it difficult for an equipped enemy to pinpoint their location via triangulation.

"Remember to force the deer into the field where we can get a shot at them instead of further into the woods. BREAK."

"Make sure you stop when I say, or I might end up plugging one of you in the dome. OVER."

There was a brief pause and Rey glanced at Kyle.

"Roger that. OVER."

"SLAUGHTER 6, OUT."

The two waited and watched.

From their vantage point they could not see where Buster and Reeves were moving as the old growth of conifer trees hid any occupants. After a half hour into the push Rey keyed his helmet microphone several times in a row as a prearranged signal to the pushers. This way if the two were in a situation where they needed to remain quiet Rey would not expose them to unwanted noise from his voice.

"5 here. OVER."

"Where you guys at? OVER."

"We're up by the northeast corner of the field, about forty to fifty meters and heading south. OVER."

"Shit. We're not seeing anything. OVER."

Rey continued to scan the field to his front as he pondered. Kyle took the binoculars he was handed earlier and searched the right side of their hunting zone. After a few moments of thinking Rey keyed the microphone again.

"Alright, look. I don't want your scent all over the trees on that far side. BREAK."

"You guys come back the way you came in and we'll sit tight here for a bit. BREAK."

"Set up a second blind position about fifty meters to our left and we'll just watch the field until evening – say about 19:00 hours. How copy? OVER."

Reynolds replied with a tired voice.

"Roger that, moving back. OVER."

"6. OUT."

Rey sighed as he removed his helmet, and with a slight tinge of disappointment looked across the rifle stock to Kyle.

"Those guys in 1st squad told me this place was a regular traffic jam of the little bastards. Where the fuck are they all?"

Kyle shrugged his shoulders and glanced behind them briefly to make sure no one was sneaking up on them. Satisfied, he continued to scan with the binoculars and the two waited in silence.

An hour later they spotted Reeves and Buster about fifty meters to the left of their hide. The two troopers gave a quick overhead wave which Rey acknowledged with one of his own. Having established visual contact the troopers assumed their own hide position and got settled in. Both teams quickly fell into a routine of watching, eating, peeing, and sleeping. It was late afternoon when Rey woke Kyle up from a cat nap.

"Hey. Wake up high speed."

Kyle squinted his aching eyes as he tried to adjust to the penetrating light. Rey turned to look back out across the field.

"I'm tired and freezing from just sitting here. Let's go for a little walk and stretch our legs."

The two collected their loose gear and headed over toward the other hide position. As they arrived at the back of the second hide Rey crawled over to explain the new plan to Reeves and Buster. Kyle was under the impression that Rey felt the two had been a little careless and spooked off the deer into the opposite direction. After a brief conversation he crawled back.

"Alright – they're going to stay here and we're going to go up through the same woods they did. Only this time we're going to swing well out to the left and make sure that any critters in there get pushed out toward the field. Once we're near the northeast corner I'll call them and have them shift their rifle to the southeast corner. We'll push down the opposite side across from where we are now. There just has to be something out here for us to bag. I don't believe those guys would jerk me around when it comes to finding food."

Kyle nodded his head and the two quietly trod off through the thinning pines to their left.

The air grew crisp and Kyle noted that the mist had long since dispersed from the small valley they had previously occupied. It would be easier for the team to be seen and heard. Kyle briefly thought about the possibility that there were no more deer in the area. Perhaps the other squads had killed enough to make the little buggers think twice before showing their cute faces again.

The pair continued to move as quietly as they could, and Kyle became aware of the wide circle Rey made as they passed through the vegetation. On the left flank of the field the trees were less of a conifer and more of a mature hardwood, providing sight range out to around thirty meters.

After pushing the trees for almost half an hour Rey signaled a quick rest. Kyle almost sighed in anticipation and strode off to a small collection of young pines to relieve his bladder.

Always hydrating means always pissing!

He slung his carbine over his shoulder, loosened his waist belt, and swung the front combat pouches out of his way. Moving up to the dense cluster of needles he fumbled with his crotch buttons as the urge to urinate became unbearable. Without warning, he stumbled upon a man already engaged in relief of his own.

The two men lock gazed for a fraction of a second before the wild man, well hidden by the deer fur he wore, gave a fierce roar and launched himself at Kyle. Taken completely by surprise the trooper was sent flailing and stumbling backward from his attacker. With his left hand the native had Kyle by the throat in a flash. His right stabbed the trooper in the heart with a wicked hunting blade.

As the knife flashed high for another strike Kyle had done the only thing he could and struggled to flip the attacker. The two rolled down into a small depression and the wild man dropped the weapon, but now employed both of his hands in a choke hold. The world flashed by in a rapid torrent of light and darkness interspersed with the smell of molding leaves as the two thrashed about.

Kyle felt himself beginning to black out as the choke hold effectively cut off his air supply. He tried to blink past the darkness that quickly pushed in from his peripheral vision but the condition only became worse. As his arms began to slacken and his lungs burned for a breath of air a final realization occurred to him.

Holy shit, this is it! I'm going to die!

The world returned to him as suddenly as it was taken.

Kyle lay motionless on his back and stared up at the empty branches reaching into the sky above him. His vision cleared from the blur of flashing light specks, and the sound of rushing blood was replaced by the wind as it blew gently from above. His body felt drained of all energy and weighed down as if filled with sand. Kyle took slow, deep breaths to feed his oxygen starved blood and he suddenly remembered his attacker.

What the hell was that all about? Where did he go?

Carefully he propped himself up and could see the man sprawled in a heap of furs on the ground next to him. Rey appeared from the left with the rifle barrel still pointed at the native. Kyle was aware that Rey spoke but he could not hear nor understand the corporal through the fog of the trauma. As if to no one in particular he asked,

"What?"

"I said 'are you alright!?' *Shit!* He was stabbing the hell out of you! Check yourself for wounds!"

Rey took a knee next to Kyle with the weapon still trained on the native. The corporal made a cursory inspection of Kyle, who sat up and checked himself by running his hands over his chest. There was no obvious sign of blood but there was a series of gashes in his left breast pocket. Kyle stuck his fingers against one of the holes and felt the copy of *Killer Angels* which caught the stabs of the blade.

Thank you Michael Shaara!

Rey kept his eyes on the man he had shot as he spoke.

"You good?"

Kyle quickly checked his arms and hands. There was a minor defensive wound on the outside of his right palm but nothing more serious. As he spoke he sounded a little slurred.

"Yeah, I'm good."

"Grab your weapon then and cover me."

Kyle forced his sluggish body to action and recovered his weapon from where it lay in the leaves a few meters away. He swept it around the area as he moved and stood in perpendicular stance to Rey.

Think clearly and keep a good line of fire. Do NOT shoot your squad leader!

Never lifting his eyes, Rey carefully circled around the attacker who remained motionless. It was obvious the corporal had no intention of repeating Kyle's mistake.

"You see anything else out there?"

Kyle looked as carefully as his fuzzed vision would allow. He searched past the swarm of zigzag blurs and it appeared that they were alone.

"I don't see anything. We seem to be clear."

"Alright then, cover me."

Rey placed his weapon against a tree and pulled his pistol from its holster. Kyle spun to point his carbine at the native and noticed the spray of blood droplets on the ground next to him. Rey carefully walked up to the furred figure and gave the man a solid kick in the thigh.

There was no response.

Rey, satisfied, holstered his weapon.

"He's not faking that – a shot like that would hurt like a mother. Keep your eyes peeled out there while I search him."

Kyle allowed his eyes to return to the terrain around them and it appeared they were still alone.

"We're still clear."

"Alright, I'm going to turn him over."

Rey grabbed the man by the ankles and rolled him over to expose dirty blonde hair and a short rough beard. His skin was weathered and tanned indicating a life spent outdoors. He was covered from head to toe in a patchwork poncho of deer fur. His eyes were closed and he appeared to be unconscious.

Rey reached down and felt for a pulse.

"SLAUGHTER 6, this is SLAUGHTER 5. OVER!"

Both Rey and Kyle jumped out of their skins as the headphones roared in their ears. Scared out of his wits Rey swore a fierce oath as he fumbled for the microphone key. Kyle carefully blew out a slow breath and calmed his already heightened nerves, aware of just how close he had come to pulling the trigger.

"SLAUGHTER 6, this is SLAUGHTER 5, OVER!!"

Rey keyed his helmet mike.

"For *fuck's sake* 5, you scared the shit out of me! What's your fucking problem? OVER."

"We've got people! We've got people in the trees! They're on the far side of the field and running!"

Rey and Kyle exchanged looks for a brief second. Kyle then dropped to one knee and scanned for the approach of targets while Rey keyed the microphone in reply.

"Which way are they heading 5? OVER."

"To the southeast from us. Was that you shooting? OVER."

Kyle relaxed a little.

Southeast means away from us. Thank god! That gives us a chance to get our shit in order before having to deal with someone else.

"Roger 5, keep an eye on them and let us know if they come back. OVER."

"Roger. OUT."

Rey felt for a pulse again on their victim and shook his head.

"He's dead."

Kyle looked again at the leaves and could now see a large puddle of bright red blood. It looked as if Rey had shot him through the side at the lower rib cage and the soft slug blew an exit hole in his flank the size of a fist. The face was that of a man asleep except it was drained of color and ashen. Kyle had to fight off the idea of similarity between this experience and that of hunting deer. Just the notion of gutting the man made him want to vomit.

Rey switched his helmet radio and tried to raise the company on the assigned frequency. After a few minutes of calling, the trooper on duty finally responded. Rey gave a contact and status report to which the operator asked for confirmation of a 'Killed In Action'.

Rey just stared at Kyle for a moment before confirming the message. They both knew that the report of an unknown KIA would spread like wildfire. The Lieutenant would definitely be interested in knowing why one of his troopers shot someone to death.

The order came back for the patrol to collect as much physical intelligence as they could. The body was to be cached until the Lieutenant could make it out to the site for a personal inspection.

Rey and Kyle quickly stripped the body of several rough metal and bone daggers. A few pouches, a small water skin, and a length of crude leather rope wrapped around a rolled hide made up the rest of the personal gear. The body looked like it was from the hills of Gaul during Roman times back on Earth. The revelation seemed to unnerve Kyle but he could not figure out why.

They wrapped the body in the rolled hide and placed it in the bottom of the shallow depression. The troopers then covered the body as best they could with dirt and leaves. After they checked for equipment or missed intelligence items, Rey quickly crossed himself and led Kyle back the way they had come. In less than twenty minutes the two linked up with Buster and Reeves and headed for home.

* * *

The patrol made it back to base in less than two hours without further incident. On entering the perimeter the four troopers were directed to report to the company command post where Lieutenant Taylor waited for them. After the orderly stepped out of the room, the Lieutenant sat back in his chair.

"What the *hell* happened out there?" he demanded in a low, curt bark.

Corporal Rey formally stepped forward and saluted.

"Sir. While conducting a hunting detail in the northern valley Private Evans stumbled onto an individual who attacked him. It was very fast and the man was extremely motivated, which forced me to shoot him or risk losing a member of my patrol. Shortly after this initial contact, Privates Buster and Reeves observed seven other individuals moving to the southeast away from the hunting location. They made no attempt to close with us and broke contact down one of the gorges. After checking on Private Evans and the other hunting team I called in my report to the company."

Rey fell silent and remained standing at attention. The Lieutenant scowled at him for a moment, squinting in the harsh over-head light.

"Stumbled? Stumbled! How the fuck does one of my infantry 'stumble' into anything?"

Rey said nothing and remained at attention. The Lieutenant shifted his glare over to Kyle who quickly snapped his eyes back to the front.

"Evans – you tripped on this guy?"

Kyle stiffened.

"Sir! I was going to relieve myself and approached a group of small dense trees. The man was already there and we surprised each other as I entered the tree line. He jumped me with a dagger and I was forced to wrestle with him. Before I knew it, Corporal Rey had shot him off me."

The Lieutenant frowned at him.

"You got jumped by a guy taking a shit?!"

"Sir, yes sir!"

Taylor leaned forward, rested his wrists on the desk in front of him and touched his finger tips together.

"Do you feel that the shooting was justified?"

For a panicked moment Kyle sensed the nervousness in Rey and knew he had to be very careful with what he said next.

"Sir, I was able to ward off the initial attack but the hostile succeeded in pinning me to the ground with a strangle hold. I was about to go unconscious when Corporal Rey shot the man off me. It is my opinion that had the Corporal not shot my attacker the man would have recovered the blade and killed me before the Corporal could have physically prevented him from doing so."

Kyle could feel the gaze of the Lieutenant studying his face for a trace of deception. It sounded almost too well thought out and for a moment the private was worried that the Lieutenant would think it was a cover story. Taylor glanced back to Rey.

"That true?"

Rey nodded quickly.

"Sir. It is my opinion that at the moment before I fired the attacker would succeed in killing Private Evans. I was not worried about the knife since Evans succeeded in disarming the man."

The Lieutenant let out a sarcastic hoot and a slight sneer appeared across his face.

"'Disarmed' my ass. The guy probably 'stumbled' over Evans and dropped it by accident."

Neither trooper said anything in response.

The Lieutenant glanced angrily over at the platoon sergeant.

"Well Holly, it appears we have infantry in this outfit that can't beat a man with his pants around his ankles in hand-to-hand combat!"

Holly stiffened and growled,

"We'll remedy that immediately, sir. Evans will report to me tomorrow morning and I will instruct him – personally."

This declaration stunned Kyle but appeared to placate the officer. Prior to the whole incident, it seemed the Lieutenant was conscious of Holly as the most experienced soldier in the company. The whole back and forth dialogue was more of a show for the two troopers than anything else.

I'm pretty sure the last person in this unit the LT wants to alienate is the Master Sergeant.

The Lieutenant turned to Rey.

"You enjoy shooting that man today?"

Rey seemed to stiffen at the veiled accusation.

How the hell would Rey possibly enjoy killing another person? What kind of an asshole would ask such a thing?

Rey took a moment to compose himself and spoke in a deliberate fashion.

"Sir. I did what I thought was my duty. If I could have captured that man without risking Private Evans I would have. He tried to kill one of my men and I was forced to shoot him. Sir."

The Lieutenant seemed to hear the resolute tone in Rey's response and nodded his head absently. He looked again at Kyle and asked,

"How do you feel about what this man did for you?"

Kyle stiffened and his mind went blank.

How do I feel?

"Sir, I'm grateful, sir."

The Lieutenant growled,

"I don't want you grateful Private, I want you trained. Make sure you get with the program so the next time you subdue the son of a bitch yourself and your squad leader doesn't have to murder someone to bail you out!"

Kyle felt a mix of anger and shame.

What the fuck do you want from me? I barely got out of that one alive!

Lieutenant Taylor picked up some papers on his desk and addressed the group as a whole.

"My compliments on the fast thinking and action of Corporal Rey. It's not an easy decision and Lord knows I've never been faced with it myself. I just want it understood that we capture where possible as these people are harder to question once they're *dead.*"

The Lieutenant glared at Kyle.

"Not to mention that it's a load off of the conscience. Regardless, a letter of commendation will go into Corporal Rey's permanent file. "

Rey muttered a reply,

"Yes, sir."

"Alright, fine. Drop your recovered intelligence items on the S2's desk and make sure that we know where that body was buried. If it's still quiet out there tomorrow we'll send a detail to bring it back. Once we've got all we need to know we'll give that bastard a proper burial."

He turned to Holly and gestured in the general direction of the four troopers.

"Master Sergeant, these cowboys are going back out tomorrow at o' dark thirty to lead the recovery patrol to the body and to serve as the litter team to carry it back."

"Yes, sir."

"Dismissed."

Their eyes went to Holly who motioned them out the door with a jerk of his head. With great relief all the troopers saluted and exited the office. Once the team was a safe distance away from prying ears Buster spoke up.

"Don't worry about it Evans. Shit happens."

Kyle looked at Buster but could not tell if it was a failed attempt at humor. His pride burned with a slow, steady humiliation and he had done his best to boost himself out of it. Kyle looked to Rey and spoke up.

"Thank you for what you did for me Corporal. I appreciate it."

Rey seemed to mull over the comment as they walked a short distance before he replied,

"Forget it. The way things are looking around here we're all going to have blood on our hands before any of this is over."

That night the whole squad cleaned its gear and prepared for the recovery patrol in the morning. They talked in hushed tones about what had happened with the other members in the squad bay until Master Sergeant Holly appeared in the doorway. At this, they all fell silent and Rey hopped up out of his seat for a brief conversation before the senior man left.

When the group was sure he was gone, a much quieter conversation continued. Kyle was glad to note the others in his platoon did not joke about his near death experience. To his relief, most of the troopers seemed proud to have an actual veteran now leading the squad. Rey did not offer what the conversation with Holly was about and no one asked.

Next morning the recovery patrol left the perimeter while it was still dark. Lieutenant Taylor accompanied the patrol as Rey, with the original hunting team, led the way. Sixteen troopers made up the column including the Lieutenant, Corporal Kelly, three fire teams of four men, and a light machinegun with a crew of two. Kyle had no idea what kind of trouble the Lieutenant expected to find but had no complaints about the extra firepower that came along for the ride.

The patrol slowly wound its way up a parallel path following the same stream bed used on the previous mission. The rest breaks were frequent, if brief, as the Lieutenant had a bug up his ass about getting to the site. An hour and a half later the exhausted and sore patrol arrived behind the hide positions the hunting team had originally occupied.

From there Reynolds and Buster answered questions about the small group they had seen across the field and showed the direction in which they had departed. After a few more questions the patrol was on its feet again plodding along the edge of the field toward the scene of the crime.

As they approach the exact location Kyle kept his eyes on the small group of trees where he had stumbled onto his assailant. Circling around it, he ensured the spot was clear of hostiles and led the others into a defensive perimeter. Rey met with the Lieutenant where the body had been cached no more than eight hours ago. The officer gave the corporal a hard look.

"You're certain it was stashed here?"

Rey nodded his head while he inspected a disturbed pile of dirt and debris at the bottom of the shallow depression. He held up several leaves stained with large amounts of dried blood for the commander to inspect. Corporal Kelly walked up after a brief inspection of the surrounding terrain.

"No scavenger dragged him away that I can tell. No scrape marks and no sign of feeding near here as there'd still be parts of the carcass or bone left over."

Lieutenant Taylor looked at the low spot and brushed aside some of the leaves with his boot to look at a pool of dried blood.

"Well, someone came and took him away. Any man who bled out that much would not even be able to crawl too far on his own."

It occurred to Kyle that the locals could be watching them at that very moment. The others seemed to get the same idea and began to scan their surroundings more thoroughly. Every shape and sound was suspect as the troopers barely dared to breathe.

A few moments later the Lieutenant got to his feet and turned back toward the way they had come.

"Either way we're done here. Keep your eyes open for evidence or other physical intelligence and let's get back to the post. We'll see about sending out some patrols in the direction you last saw them fleeing."

Rey looked to Kyle who could only shrug in reply. As best the two could tell they were indeed in the correct location. There was simply no denying the fact that the body was gone.

The two started out after Lieutenant Taylor and the rest of the men fell into a tactical column. The machinegun crew bitched quietly under their breath at having to lug the gun all the way out there for nothing. Such was life.

The entire trip home Kyle could not shake the feeling that they had been watched.

* * *

CHAPTER III

"Alright, try it again."

Every muscle of Kyle's body ached. He was just plain exhausted. In truth, he was not just tired but very bruised as well. His face hurt and his skin was excoriated from his succeeding imbroglio. They had been at it for over an hour and Holly had not looked the least bit winded.

I wish I could say 'you should see the other guy'!

The older man sat cross-legged on the ground wearing a blindfold. He remained motionless, listening for Kyle to approach. Ever since the shooting, hand-to-hand skills training had been the priority on training schedules for Kyle and the rest of the company.

Kyle took a step forward.

"Stop."

Kyle froze as Holly removed his blindfold and got to his feet.

"Son, you really need to start paying attention. Look at your feet. I can tell by sound alone that you crossed your leg over your centerline, thus limiting your range of movement and response."

Kyle looked down and saw that it was true. The senior man continued.

"I know you're tired and I know I've been kicking your ass all over this parade ground but you need to dig down deep and do a gut check. If Corporal Rey hadn't been there you'd be a prisoner or, more likely, dead right now. You need to reach into that soft inner core and make some steel on the outside or one day you're going to get yourself and possibly others killed."

Kyle felt a wave of defeat come over him.

Alright Evans, knock off the cry baby shit! This is what he is talking about! You need to step up to the plate and do the job or you're gonna die!

The platoon sergeant was not trying to make him feel bad by putting him down and this Kyle knew. He had honestly thought of himself as a good soldier and, yet, he was very disappointed by his own lack of ability. It had not helped that several guys in the sister platoons made wisecracks about the incident - as if it were anything to laugh at. But he had seen a look of regard in the eyes of some of the others in the company. They stared at him as if he were supposed to be dead. Some looked with pity, others with scorn.

Let them get jumped and nearly beat to death and see how they like it.

"Let's do this one more time and let's get it right."

Kyle nodded his head and Holly suddenly launched a flying tackle. Kyle forced himself to hold some air in his lungs and let the rest go, anticipating impact with the ground. As soon as they landed, he frantically tried to flip the larger man over using the momentum of the fall to help with the throw. He was partially successful.

Ignoring that this was the most experienced killer in the company, Kyle began to pummel and knee Holly with all his might. He felt a few good blows land and, as a result, a brief moment of hope. A second later Kyle was caught by the wrist, painfully twisted askew, and saw stars as the wind was knocked out of him for the fifteenth time that day. He lay in a heap trying to catch his breath while coughing up dust from the scuffle.

You had him there for a second, Evans - at least I think you did.

Breathing hard he waited for the flashing lights to pass from his vision. As the burning in his lungs began to ease Holly suddenly loomed into view. Kyle instinctively shielded his face with his arms and cocked his legs to receive the attack.

Nothing happened.

The Master Sergeant was panting with his hand resting on his upper leg for support. Kyle noticed a trickle of blood from his nose and Holly appeared to be wincing from a hit to his groin.

Oh my god - he's going to kill me!

Panting, the older man just breathed heavily with a large grin which largely concealed the unmistakable look of pain on his face.

"Alright! Now that's... what... I'm talking about..."

Laughing, Holly reached down and offered his hand to Kyle who was hesitant to accept it. Realizing it was not a trick the young trooper was returned to his feet. Holly wiped the blood off his own face with the back of his hand and stood up as straight as his injury would allow. It seemed that in the mad scramble Kyle had indeed managed to get a knee in somewhere.

"I'm real sorry about that Master Sergeant..."

Holly laughed again with the same wide grin on his face and exhaled deeply.

"Hell no son, you did real good on that one. Anything worth fighting for is worth fighting dirty for. I'm just glad that we found something in there that was willing to fight. It will take a little more repetition to make the training instinctive, but this is a sign that there is hope for you. Go get cleaned up and grab some food. Tell Corporal Rey that you have light duty for the next twenty-four hours."

Kyle straightened painfully into the position of parade rest.

"Roger that Master Sergeant."

Holly nodded his head and simply turned away, at which point Kyle slumped considerably. With an exhausted limp he headed back across the central parade ground toward the squad bay.

The guys are never going to believe I actually kneed that man.

The company post had evolved beneath thick overhead branches of large pine trees. In the weeks following the sighting of the locals, the troopers had worked regular fatigue details fortifying earthen positions and digging new facilities.

The fruit of their labor was a sunken village located several feet below the surface of the woods which contained communication trenches, fighting bunkers, living quarters, and general services. Excavated dirt was placed to form a low camouflaged wall around the entire perimeter with a reinforced inner lattice made from woven cut saplings. The improvement provided additional cover and concealment within the fort and reduced exposure of troopers to direct observation.

The drop ships took turns and sat in high orbit for durations of up to a week while they conducted surface mapping and long range space scans. Rumor had it the initial results detected a large energy wave moving away from the planet as it dissipated. According to calculations from the super computer the originating point of this wave was from orbit and initiated at almost the same moment as the insertion Fold of the *Rosalie*.

What had created the wave was unknown but wild speculation suggested that enemy had a new capability to lasso Fold destinations with the intent to then ambush their victims. The suggested rational for their own survival was that the lone enemy ship had bit off more than it could chew when it pulled in a midget carrier.

Corporal Rey rejected this theory when he shared a conversation he had with one of the drop ship crew chiefs. According to the chief, the enemy ship would have had to of been a hundred times larger than it was in order to generate an effect powerful enough to interfere with the astrophysical forces involved with a Fold. More probable, what ever diverted the *Rosalie* also snagged the other vessel at the same time and the attack was primarily an alarmed reflex. The fact that the remaining drop ships were not sought out and destroyed seemed to bear this theory out. Who or what might have brought both vessels to this unknown planet still remained a mystery.

Kyle often thought about what it would have been like had enemy ships slid into orbit over head and pounded the base with their weaponry. Even though the living quarters and defensive positions were a couple of meters below the forest floor they did little to comfort anyone who knew what modern weaponry could do. The small cannon of ancient cruisers from several centuries ago would have been sufficient to turn Kyle and his fellow troopers into a smoking crater one hundred meters across and thirty meters deep.

His aching body brought Kyle's thoughts back to the present and the task at hand. He knew the pain would get worse over the next few days as the bruises healed and the muscle mended. His only remedy was to stretch a lot and suck up the aches and pains until the healing process ran its course. Kyle grinned to himself.

I need to talk to Rey about making an improvised hot tub. What I need use is a nice long soak!

With his thoughts lost in a daydream Kyle failed to notice a group of troopers off to the left as they scrambled out of their underground quarters and into the trenches which led to their assigned fighting positions. As Kyle entered the trench to his squad area a trooper appeared up ahead and called out a warning to make way.

Standing aside, Kyle was amused to observe the guy race past with his helmet and web gear askew. He watched long enough to see the man disappear down an adjacent corridor that led toward the company headquarters area.

Oops! Late for Charge of Quarters duty! He'll get his ass chewed for sure!

Turning back to continue down the trench Kyle was almost bowled over by a trio of troopers from the 1st Squad. They moved with a determined seriousness that piqued his interest.

Something's up. Those guys are rushing somewhere.

Two more troopers emerged from his platoon area and Kyle called out as they rushed past.

"Hey! What's going on?"

"Better get to your position! We've got visitors on the perimeter!"

The trooper disappeared with his buddy trailing behind, still trying to pull his web gear over body armor. Kyle sprinted the remaining distance down the trench to his squad bay and equipment. As he rounded the last corner Kyle came across Sergeant Walther, the 1st Squad Leader, who was directing a group of his troopers. He glanced briefly toward Kyle as he dispatched the men to their assigned duties.

"Evans! Grab your shit and report to Rey on the double!"

Kyle nodded his head in acknowledgement and disappeared into the buried storage container which was now home to the squad. He quickly dropped his physical training gear onto the bunk and pulled on his combat uniform. Next he slid on his torso body armor while leaving the upper arm shield straps loose.

Sitting down on the bunk he pulled on his calf length boots and snapped the quick-bindings shut. The equipment load-bearing web vest went on next and Kyle placed the carbine strap over his head and slung the weapon across his back. Upon leaving, he grabbed his helmet from the wall hook and donned it. Moving as quickly as possible he straightened and then tightened the chin strap. A million thoughts raced through his head.

Who the hell is it? What do they want? Are they from this planet or are they from orbit?

Kyle clipped the last of his gear as he stumbled into Corporal Rey who was coming to the doorway of the bunker. Rey caught Kyle and steadied him against the wall.

"Easy killer! Where have you been? I've been calling for you for the last five minutes."

Kyle pointed to the bruise on his cheek.

"I was with Holly getting my ass beat."

"Squad frequency has changed to fife-two fife-fife. Make the switch and give me a radio check."

Kyle did as he was told and Rey gave him the okay. The corporal turned and gestured to a smaller trench that branched off to the right of the current position.

"The rest of the fire team is down on the right hand side of the line and tied in with the 1st Platoon positioned to your right flank. You're sharing a hole with Buster and serving as the assistant gunner. Make sure you guys have your eyes peeled and report anything you see as soon as you see it."

"You got it Corporal."

Kyle hustled the remaining distance to the fighting position and startled a jumpy Buster.

"For fuck's sake Evans!"

Kyle grinned to himself.

I don't have to say it do I Buster? Looks like I'm not the only one who can get surprised around here!

Buster returned to checking his weapon and prepared the bricks of projectiles for firing. The two were about the same age and had served in the same rifle company since Basic. Almost two years spent together, they were more or less brothers of a very large family. Without looking away from his task, he asked Kyle in a curt tone.

"Where the hell you been?"

Buster stacked the remaining projectile bricks for the light machinegun. Kyle shifted into his own firing position and adjusted his combat load to make himself more comfortable. He glanced out of the aperture and noted nothing of interest outside the immediate perimeter. He then focused his attention on the distant pine trees which were located over a hundred meters away.

"Holly was giving me some dancing tips."

Buster flashed a condescending smirk.

"More like he's been kicking the shit out of you."

Buster glanced up from his machinegun and scanned their assigned field of fire. Kyle shifted himself slightly and moved an ammo brick which dug into his side. Although able to find a comfortable firing posture Kyle felt his muscles warm with pain from the training lesson.

"I didn't do so bad today. Gave him a little nose bleed. You'd be surprised how fast and strong he is."

Buster glanced over at him with a cocked eyebrow.

"No I wouldn't. You know he used to be with the Special Forces back during the Riots?"

Kyle had not been privy to that information before, however, he only shrugged his shoulders. He figured everyone had to come from somewhere, but the Riots had been some of the stickiest operations conducted in recent history. If Holly walked out of that mess in one piece then he definitely earned another notch of respect as far as Kyle was concerned.

"It's not so bad. I'll tell him you want lessons too."

Kyle grinned to himself as he knew this would needle the machine gunner.

"I just might if you're finally able to go to the shitter without a baby sitter anymore."

Buster looked smug as he scanned the ground to their front. Kyle was used to the ribbing by now as they had plenty of practice together. Having formally exchanged ideas, there was only one thing left to say.

"Hey Buster…"

"Yeah?"

"Go fuck yourself."

Buster chuckled quietly but never took his eyes off the distant trees. In a way being like brothers could be just as annoying, but it had its good points too. Buster had picked a fight with another trooper who made some off hand comment about Kyle getting jumped in the woods. In a close knit family you were allowed to rib your own but heaven help the outsider who violated protocol. Either way, Kyle changed the subject to anything but brooding over what had happened that day.

"What's everybody getting all excited about?"

Buster shrugged his shoulders and gestured with his head toward the dense tree line in the distance.

"Rey said that one of the security patrols caught sight of a large body of natives heading this way from the southeast. I thought I saw something by the base of those pines a few minutes ago but I haven't seen much else since. Whoever they are, they seem to be spread out along our entire perimeter from the southeast to down here."

Kyle came up behind Buster and observed over his shoulder the spot in question. If these people were in fact gathered as Buster said, then that meant there had to be at least a couple of hundred to cover the ground sufficiently. The general feeling was that the trees held something, although Kyle knew it could just be his overactive imagination. Ever since the company had made landfall it was hard to shake the feeling that they were under constant observation. There were even rumors about small black shadows that would appear in the trees and disappear with the blink of an eye.

Rey approached the entrance to the fighting position and quickly inspected the bunker for readiness. He appeared satisfied at seeing grenades and the command detonated mine triggers where they should be according to Standard Operating Procedure.

Buster turned and sat against the bunker wall.

"Hey Rey, what's up out there?"

Rey shrugged slightly.

"Company says the fellows are in furs and carrying flags and spears. Looks like the Bronze Age has arrived to kick our sorry asses."

Buster snorted and raised an eyebrow.

"No shit."

Rey revealed the slightest hint of a smile.

"Okay, listen up. Word from higher up is to wound, not kill."

Buster glanced over at Kyle with an incredulous expression on his face.

"What?! Are you fucking kidding me? You're joking, right?"

He looked at Rey who simply shook his head.

Kyle persisted,

"What happened to the time honored tradition of 'Kill! Kill! Kill we will'?"

Rey looked out past them through the firing slit toward the distant trees. Kyle noted how their squad leader seemed unaffected by the endless sarcasm. The corporal always appeared to remain calm and collected despite having to deal with the agitating comments of his subordinates. Kyle had learned from childhood to emulate the qualities that he admired in others. It was good the team had someone like Rey to look out for them.

If I had to deal with jokers like us I'd be ripping my hair out by now.

"The Lieutenant wants to reduce blowback if we have to shoot these people. If we can manage to wound them then we can help them and be best buddies. If we wax them, their families will probably swear some sort of blood feud and they'll never stop trying to kill us. We still have no idea when the extraction is going to come and take us off the planet so he figures we need all the friends we can get."

Kyle thought about that for a brief moment.

Does Rey think this has something to do with that guy he shot? If so what does this mean for him?

Rey continued.

"If it's the local welcoming committee or ends up being someone with sufficient firepower, I'll pass you the kill order and you can bag as many of the bastards as you can. If you see a visual signal of three green star shell clusters fired over them then it's the signal to start killing. But keep in mind that the LT isn't looking to have to report to his superior that we gunned down a bunch of backwards people armed with fur and pointy sticks."

Kyle thought of the dead man again.

If I hadn't had that paperback in my pocket that guy would have killed me. Pointy stick my ass, Higher can go to hell.

Kyle was vexed by the shooting. He was tired of worrying about what would happen as a result of the surprise encounter. Even though Rey had the blood on his hands Kyle knew his own upset was due to what the Lieutenant had said. Regardless, the ruling was that the killing was justified and any future board of inquiry would have to take that into account.

Wouldn't they? Then again with how the military functions, I should expect to be stood up in front of a firing squad!

Rey continued speaking and pulled Kyle back to the present.

"So the deal is that we are to keep the shots below the knees and take them in the leg where possible. If, for whatever reason, there is no one in the chain of command present and you find either yourself or a fellow trooper in a life threatening situation then, and only then, are you authorized to use lethal force."

Rey looked them both in the eyes to make sure the instructions sank in.

"But I warn you, make sure it is justified or the Lieutenant is going to skin you alive. Off the record, if you have to pull the trigger on someone like that, make sure you're the only one left breathing to file a statement. Understood?"

Both troopers nodded their heads. Kyle had never heard dark humor from Rey before.

Then again he's been there and he doesn't seem to be joking.

"Good luck."

The two troopers gave a low grunt and Rey backed out of the bunker. Buster turned back to observe their zone. Kyle noted the carbine strapped across his back. During action this locale kept the weapon accessible yet out of the way. If they had to abandon the fighting position there was no chance it would get left behind. For the majority of the fighting he and Buster would be responsible for keeping the light machinegun in action. Buster spoke out loud so Kyle could hear.

"I hope they do come after us. I'm getting tired of hiding in holes from dip-shits dressed up like animals."

Kyle nodded absently as he pulled the bolt on his carbine and observed the projectile entering the feed chamber. He slid the bolt forward until it stripped the shot from the ammo brick and locked it into the breech from where it would be fired.

The beauty of the weapons was that they were powered by a compression chamber similar to a child's air rifle; the difference being that the fired projectile could penetrate one centimeter of rolled steel plate at ten meters. Without the need for a controlled explosion to propel the shots, the carbine was a hard weapon to locate and the soldier never ran out of propellant. The weapons could even fire underwater where the only difference in performance was due to the friction of water, which, in effect, was noticeable only outside of short range.

Standard issue prefabricated projectile was the only limitation of a sustained battle. The composition of the shot was what generated the penetrating power. The stock of the weapon could shape improvised projectiles in a pinch. Various materials could be utilized, but nothing performed quite like tungsten core metallic projectiles. Nevertheless, it was amusing to watch an instructor drop targets at fifty meters using only the dirt at his feet.

There's more than one way to skin a cat!

Turning back to his firing position, Kyle shifted several of the grenades and mine triggers to one side to ensure they were kept out of the way. If Rey wanted the bad guys taken alive then the mass casualty weapons had to be held until the last possible moment. Not withstanding, Kyle had every intention of blowing those jackasses to hamburger if he had to.

Somehow I think I'll manage to live with the guilt.

Staring out through the mono wire protecting the perimeter Kyle waited to see what happened next. The extremely narrow material glinted like spider silk in the sun but could inconveniently slice into anything forced against it. A bad guy running through at full speed could amputate, castrate, and decapitate himself before he knew what was happening. A trooper handling the material almost lost a finger just trying to help string it up.

For thirty minutes Kyle and Buster held a low conversation while they kept their eyes fixed on the distant tree line. After a while the constant scanning got to Kyle and his eyes began to tire. Reaching back, he pulled a canteen from his web harness for a drink of water.

A sudden roar from perhaps hundreds of deep, angry voices echoed out from behind the distant trees in a long and continuous drone. Kyle and Buster both froze trying to comprehend the sound. Their eyes met for a brief moment as they both gauged what they were hearing. To Kyle, the sound was reminiscent of only a few weeks past.

It's them! It has to be! They sound really frigging pissed off!

His gut tightened. He remembered the fierce attack of the wild man who had choked him nearly to death. Out there were hundreds, if not thousands, of men just like him. They could be family. Kyle knew that they were armed to the teeth and wanting to hurt someone. He felt a cold fear stir in the tightness of his gut.

Can they possibly know about the shooting? Could they be looking for Rey, or even me?

"Hey Buster, you can make fun of me all you want but whatever you do, don't let one of those bastards get a hand on you."

Buster braced himself behind the machinegun.

"You got that right."

Kyle might not have been king of the hand-to-hand crap Holly tried to beat into his head, but he sure as hell could shoot the shit out of anyone who dared to charge at him. If he could have taught the newcomers anything it would have been that you don't bring a spear to a gun fight. Their helmet headphones briefly crackled with static as someone keyed the squad frequency.

"Alright! Get ready…"

It was Rey.

"Like I said, the LT wants these guys alive. They have no idea what they are up against so take your shots as quickly and methodically as possible. Every shot counts. Keep them low and try not to hit anyone who has already fallen wounded. If I find out one of you guys killed someone unnecessarily I'm going to tell your mothers and they'll have your balls."

Kyle rolled his eyes and shook his head.

Again with the mothers.

Rey continued.

"Bravo Team, you guys work from right to left in your sector. Buster will start from the flank of the enemy advance and thin out the ranks with sustained bursts across the whole front. Evans will follow behind the machinegun and pick off the remaining individuals in order to keep them from flanking us to the right. You are not to allow anyone to make it to the 1st Platoon sector to your right. Understood?"

Both Kyle and Buster keyed their microphones and acknowledged the instructions. To the other fire team located off to the left,

"Calhoun will mirror Buster but work from left to right with Reeves playing copycat to Evans. You guys in Alpha Team need to make sure that any fire from you overlaps 2nd Squad to your left. BREAK."

The two troopers from Alpha keyed their helmet microphones and acknowledged the orders. Speaking to all of them Rey continued,

"If we get the Final Protective Fire signal, get your heads down and click off your mines. Remember, the visual signal is three red star shell clusters. BREAK."

"With the 'all clear' you start shooting to kill anyone who is still a threat inside of the wire. That will be three white star shell clusters. Hopefully it won't come to that, but we'll have to see how much headway these guys make and how many of them there are. BREAK."

When Rey spoke again his voice was steady and controlled.

"Remember to keep it cool, guys. Just relax and think of it as another day on the firing range. Remind yourself out load to 'aim low' and go for below the knees before you fire or you'll end up getting center of mass hits like you were trained. OVER."

All troopers in the fire team keyed their mikes and acknowledge the directive. Kyle shook his head with building frustration. He had fired thousands of projectiles for the last two years with the mantra 'shoot to kill' etched into his brain. Now it was 'shoot to wound him in the leg' on a moments notice.

Frigging army. Wound, kill - make up your mind!

The roaring from the trees continued for a minute and then abruptly stopped. A dead quiet fell over the entire field and distant trees. Although he could not see them, Kyle knew there were other firing positions all around the perimeter filled with troopers just like him. He wondered how many of them were already squeezing their triggers and if they were just as scared as he was.

Another roar, louder than the first, came from the distant trees. In one massive body, a wall of warriors burst forth from the dense underbrush at a full sprint. Kyle felt his heart leap in his chest at the sight of the hundreds of wild men heading straight for him.

Holy shit! Here they come!

A few banners fluttered as they came off to the left and a shining gleam of light from hand weapons made for an impressive display. Sprinkled in amongst the crowd was the occasional round-shield and a few helmets with horns protruding toward the front. Kyle found himself more in awe than afraid until the sound of Rey brought him back to reality.

"Okay guys! Remember, have a good firing posture. Make sure you stay within your sector stakes and keep good coverage on your area of responsibility. Take your weapon off of safe and wait for my command."

Kyle leaned against the wall of the bunker and pulled the carbine tight to his shoulder. He let his forward grip lay limp on a cut log and cradled the weapon gently in his hand. Except for the urge to piss himself, it felt very much like a day at the firing range.

Further down on the left there was scattered carbine fire.

Rey kept tight fire control over his two teams.

"Nervous troopers firing too soon. Don't be like that. Keep your aim low and pay attention while you shoot."

If I wasn't trying so hard to make out their legs I'd probably be shooting too.

The warriors screamed as they ran at full speed with no sign of faltering. Kyle noted that there could be a thousand of them. The natives continued to close the distance between them. Kyle remembered the last time he had to sprint a hundred meters in his combat armor and marveled at their stamina.

"….Ready…."

Kyle tightened his sight picture and selected his first target. The man was slightly taller than the rest and swung a hand axe over his head. He focused in on the man and remembered to go for the lower legs.

"….Aim….."

His vision began to blur and individual legs were impossible to make out in the shifting grass and glare of shining weapons.

I'm about to open a can of whoop ass on some Vikings!

"…aim low….FIRE!"

Buster opened up with a long burst from the light machinegun. Gunners were trained to be the first and last into action in order to achieve and maintain fire superiority. At the rate Buster fired he would need every last brick of the projectiles he had set out earlier.

Kyle focused back in on his target again. It was not a man but a target. It had no family, friends, or feelings. Kyle took up his sight picture again, aimed low and squeezed until the recoil of the weapon surprised him.

CRACK!

His eyes flew wide open and he saw the target as it tumbled to the ground.

I hope I didn't just kill you!

As he aimed lower, Kyle picked out the next in line.

Squeeze, squeeze, squeeze, squeeze, squeeze…

CRACK!

Buster fired in long bursts; to Kyle the rapid succession of shots became a background to his own effort.

PACK-ACK-ACK-ACK-ACK-ACK-ACK-ACK!

For a moment Kyle heard other firing elsewhere. He took up the next warrior who charged into his sights.

CRACK!

Down he went.

CRACK!

And another.

CRACK!

And another.

As the last target fell into the tall grass Kyle risked a quick glance at the rest of the mass of men who pressed in on the left flank. Along the entire line, holes gaped as enemy troops dropped like flies. The untouched enemy pressed the attack and sprinted at a full yell.

These guys are unbelievable! They just keep coming!

Slightly rushed, Kyle dropped back into his firing position and took up the next target. He barely remembered to drop his aim before he squeezed the trigger.

CRACK!

The target went down hard and Kyle took aim on the next victim. To himself he muttered out loud,

"Aim low."

CRACK!

Nothing. Kyle tightened his shot picture and went for the knees.

CRACK!

The warrior went down and the next one appeared in his sights.

CRACK!

CRACK!

CRACK!

CRACK!

Kyle frantically scanned his sector for another target but there was no one in front of him. He realized with a rush of relief that the attack on their front had been broken.

PACK-ACK-ACK-ACK-ACK-ACK-ACK-ACK!

Buster popped off the last burst and Kyle strained to see further to the left of their position. The entire field, for as far as he could see, was littered with writhing bodies. Some of the warriors limped and tried to stand on their remaining good limbs. Others lay there with their heads occasionally bobbing up before falling back to the ground in pain.

The entire enemy charge was ruined.

Kyle laughed out loud to himself. Buster suddenly leaned back from the machinegun with a huge grin on his face. The two gave a joyous whoop and started cheering to release the stark fear that had clung to their bodies. Kyle was the first to speak.

"Did you see that? Did you see that?"

"Yeah man, get some!"

Buster let out another wild whoop.

"Did you see them come? Straight at us man! Straight at us!"

Kyle nodded his head with relief written all over his face. Between them, the two had just mowed down several dozen enemy. Kyle was surprised at how numb he felt.

So much for noble combat.

A moment of guilt passed quickly, and he was just glad to be alive and breathing. The squad sat in their positions and slowly a cross chatter started between the holes on the radio. Buster had the gall to claim around a hundred casualties by himself. Rey cut into the conversation and reminded the gunners to check their ammo loads. He also told the rest of the teams to keep their eyes peeled for another push. Reeves muttered something about the counting ability of machine gunners and their poor eyesight. Rey cut in again,

"Hey, can it guys; we've got a fragmentary order. Reeves and Evans report to Sergeant Walther at the platoon assembly area. You're going out to secure prisoners and help haul wounded."

What?!

Kyle had not liked the idea of leaving the fighting position. After all that time making it nice and safe and now they had ordered him out of it. Buster was up in arms about being left to stay put.

"What?! Why the hell do I have to stay here?! Have Evans stay here and I'll go instead!"

Rey chimed back over the headphones.

"We have to continue to provide perimeter security and you're the man with the area defense weapon. Quit your belly aching and watch the trees on the far side of the field. The aid and litter teams may be coming back in a hurry if there is anyone else out there. Unless, of course, you want to give up your gunner slot to Evans, then you can be his assistant instead."

Buster just looked out of the firing window with disgust.

"Besides, they're probably going to end up carrying those bastards in on litters all day, in full combat armor, while you get to sit here in your nice hole waiting for more bad guys to show up so you can shoot them."

That appeared to placate the gunner, who looked over at Kyle.

"Fine. You bitches have fun."

Kyle shook his head and policed up his grenades before filing out of the position to join up with Reeves. He secured the grenades in carry pouches on his vest and hurried to keep up with the others who moved out ahead of him.

As the group filtered down to the platoon area it grew by several more before finally reaching Sergeant Walther. The man was still giving instructions in six different directions but appeared to have the situation under control. To Kyle, it appeared as though the sergeant had never stopped since last time he saw the man. He and Reeves were quickly directed to carry a few of the folding litters and they fell in behind one of the company medics. After a brief headcount the party continued down to the wire passage point. Beyond the narrow opening in the mono wire lay the field sprinkled with enemy.

The Lieutenant gathered them up.

"Alright! Listen up!"

The gaggle of troopers and medics fell silent. Holly stood to the right and behind the lieutenant with his arms crossed. His eyes briefly met with Kyle's before they continued on. Once satisfied he had their complete attention, Lieutenant Taylor proceeded.

"These guys were pissed, pumped, and ready to kill you. Now they're on the ground bleeding and in a lot of pain. Do not let them get the drop on you. Do not allow yourself to be stabbed by some meat head who doesn't know when he is beat."

The Lieutenant glanced at Kyle and the trooper simply gazed back.

Don't worry about me sir, I've got it covered.

"You will protect the docs with your lives. You will wait for orders from a sergeant before you do anything. The only standing order is that if we come under attack in the field you fall back to the passage point and the defensive positions while the firing line covers you. Do not stay out there, and shoot back if the order to withdraw is given. Don't give the enemy a covered approach up through our wire."

Kyle thought about trigger happy Buster who watched over them with the machinegun. He involuntarily shuddered, as the notion of being under the barrel of the disgruntled gunner seemed like a bad place to be.

"The security teams will advance past the enemy and secure the far tree line. Once they are in place and there is no danger of a second wave, the aid and litter teams will filter out to evacuate the wounded by priority. You knuckle heads understand me?"

The body of troopers murmured a unified acknowledgement. The Lieutenant turned and nodded his head to Holly before he disappeared down the trail toward the company headquarters. Holly stepped forward and gained their attention.

"Alright boys, keep your eyes and ears open! If you see someone about to hurt one of our people, shoot them in the head until they stop moving. No games, no dicking around. Watch out for arrows or other shit that might be launched from the trees, as there may be stragglers or a unit reserve still hiding out there. We're all going out and we're all coming back. Check?"

The gathered troopers replied as one.

Kyle paired up with Reeves and the two fell into line behind one of the medics by the name of Doc Roberts. Even though Roberts was roughly the same age as they were, it was not uncommon for the medics to be treated as parental figures. When the going got tough, and a trooper had his face hanging off or guts strewn out, it was the medics who would be counted on to do whatever was necessary to try and save them. This responsibility earned them a high level of respect from the other troopers in the ranks.

The aid and litter teams advanced through the passage point in the perimeter wire with Holly counting each trooper as they stepped out. The group entered the field and automatically began to spread out from the fatal funnel they found themselves in. The security elements carefully picked their way past the piles of fallen warriors who gathered in self protective clumps. Kyle could see the carbines of the teams pointed, as a warning, toward the hostile natives. He expected a sudden lunge and a shot from the passing troopers, but nothing happened.

A large man, who wore a sort of plaid over-garment, managed to hoist himself up and stood on one good leg. Around him the arms of his fellows propped him up. Before Kyle or anyone else could utter a warning the warrior hurled a hand axe at the back of a security team that had just maneuvered past. The weapon struck one of the troopers in the back with a hard knock.

As if on cue, the air filled with flung blades and light throwing axes from the various piles of wounded men around them. Kyle and Reeves quickly positioned themselves between the natives and Doc Roberts, although a feeble axe throw was the only item which landed near them.

A voice which Kyle had not recognized came in on the left headphone. It was the frequency used by the company.

"Anyone hurt?"

A long moment passed as the various team leaders checked on their people.

"Negative."

Troopers aimed and fired at the warriors who attempted a follow up. Unlike the previous engagement, these shots were meant to kill. Kyle watched several enemy fall dead in response. There were a few angry shouts from the security elements to the natives as if daring them to make another try. Holly boomed in over the helmet head phones.

"Alright, alright, let's settle down. Forget the bravado and focus on your jobs. Get past those jokers and set up the security screen so the litter teams can get to work."

Doc Roberts turned to Kyle and Reeves.

"Alright you two, follow me."

Kyle hopped up after Doc as he veered off to the right. He tightly clutched a folded litter in one hand and had a shoulder slung carbine at the ready in the other. The medic zeroed in on one of the warriors who had been shot in the last round of firing. Kyle noticed the similarity to the man who tried to kill him and could tell that he was beyond saving even before Doc uttered a word. The wounded were now close by and groaned in pain. The team neared a larger group of natives while a sergeant gestured for them to stay back.

"Hold here Doc. These guys are pretty pissed and still full of vinegar."

The warriors were gathered in a rough circle of protection, using their bodies and shields as a barrier. A few lay motionless near the back of the pack, and it was those who Doc tried to assess, in vain, from a distance. In exasperation he vented to the sergeant.

"I can't see how bad they are, but that guy looks like he's going to kick the bucket if we don't get him help, and quick!"

Roberts took a tentative step forward and the screen of wild men either growled or waved their spears and blades. The sergeant cautioned the medic.

"Easy Doc, they get a hold of you and they'll cut off your balls."

All around, the sea of wounded seemed to go on forever. Most had long hair tied in braids sporting a thick beard or goatee. Their faces were full of pain and anger. Many were bellowing unintelligible threats and some even spit at the troopers in contempt. Kyle noted that these warriors were far from beaten in spirit even though their legs had been shot out from under them. Some, even threateningly, waved axes or swords from where they lay stretched out on their backs or sides.

Doc placed his kit bag on the ground and carefully walked toward the group of natives with his empty hands clearly visible. He spoke with a calm, clear, reassuring voice.

"Easy guys, we're here to help. We're here to help you."

One of the warriors lunged a spear thrust that was far from striking, but clearly a warning. The sergeant leveled his carbine on the man and Roberts waved him off.

"No! Wait! He wasn't anywhere near me. I'm fine. Let it go."

The sergeant lowered the weapon, clearly aggravated.

"These fucking people! Don't they understand we're trying to help?"

Doc shook his head in reply.

"They had reason enough in their minds to fight us and we shot them in the ass. I don't think they'd be too willing to believe that we're here to help them at this point. We just have to keep our cool."

The warriors continued to yell and taunt the troopers. Kyle looked at Reeves, who nervously watched another cluster of angry men. Their voices had become hoarse with the constant bellowing.

If this keeps up we're going to have a blood bath on our hands.

The sergeant continued to grow more agitated, and Roberts more frantic, as the seriously wounded natives visibly worsened. It was clear to Kyle that the warriors were not going to back down. These men would fight with their last breath to protect their wounded even when beaten. He remembered the advice of his father.

You have to do what you think is right.

At that moment Kyle knew what that was. If he tried to get permission the sergeant was sure to overrule him. It was better to later beg for forgiveness than allow the man to muddle things now.

Kyle quickly placed the folded litter on the ground at his feet and laid his carbine against it. Reaching up he unclasped his helmet chin strap. Reeves glanced over and looked nervously back to the mass of natives. In a harsh whisper the scared trooper asked,

"Evans, what the hell are you doing?"

Kyle ignored him and placed the helmet on the ground. Reaching up he unclipped the keepers to his battle vest and released the catch on his body armor.

I have to get this off before the sergeant notices me or its game over.

Dropping his battle vest and armor to the ground Kyle reached down and pulled off his undershirt, baring his chest. Rarely exposed to the light of day for the past several months, his skin had remained a pasty white beneath his uniform and body armor.

The better for them to see.

Reeves looked confused and placed his own litter to the ground so he could take better hold of his carbine. Nervously he scanned the natives.

Kyle tried not to block the line of fire from the trooper in case some of the crazier natives came after him. He pulled his bayonet from its sheath and walked up behind Doc where the sergeant finally noticed him. The shock and anger that registered on the face of the latter were plain to see.

"What the FUCK do you think you're doing?!"

Doc turned and stared at the trooper who was stripped to the waist and holding the bayonet. Kyle looked nervously back at the medic, silently pleading for Roberts to understand what he was trying to do.

This is the only way. They're never going to yield in time.

Understanding dawned on Roberts and he stepped aside to allow Kyle to move forward where the wounded natives could clearly see him. Kyle held the bayonet high so that the blade was visible to his now silent audience. The sergeant started to utter something but Roberts quickly silenced him with a motion of his hand. Doc then nodded to Kyle who took a deep, calming breath.

Okay, here goes nothing!

In one slow motion Kyle dragged the edge of the blade across his chest from above his heart down to the lowermost right rib. He could feel the burn as the razor sliced effortlessly though his skin. Kyle kept focused in order to cut deeply enough to draw blood, but not so deep as to eviscerate himself. The sergeant stared at him in stunned disbelief.

"Holy… fucking…. shit…"

With the cut completed Kyle tried to determine if it was sufficiently deep without taking his eyes off his audience. They all stared at his torso and waited. Kyle took a slow, deep breath and held it. The burn increased across the whole length of the cut and a thin, crimson line appeared in stark contrast to the white skin which surrounded it. As the blood began to slowly ooze out of the cut, Kyle took the flat of the blade and gently spread the bright red substance. Having done this he twisted slowly for all of the silent warriors to see the wound. Every last set of eyes locked on him with intense curiosity. Without turning his head Kyle spoke over his shoulder to Roberts.

"Hey Doc? You think you can make a big show of bandaging me up for these guys to see?"

Roberts stepped up beside Kyle and pulled out a can of spray skin, careful not to block the view of the audience. He sprayed on the numbing agent mixed with elastic sulfa which would stop the bleeding and protect the wound.

Roberts then held up a piece of gauze bandage for the warriors to see before he wrapped it ceremoniously across the cut. The medic took Kyle by the hand and began to shake it in a slow and exaggerated manner.

"Smile Evans, smile. Look the happiest you've ever looked in your whole miserable life."

Kyle broke out in a huge forced smile and the two gave the most obnoxiously jovial laugh they could manage. Kyle asked Roberts,

"You think they get it?"

Roberts replied through a faux grin of his own.

"There's only one way to find out."

He looked down at the compromised warrior who was positioned amongst the group. Kyle slowly moved forward as the eyes of those surrounding the fallen man cautiously turned and looked at one native in particular within their midst. Kyle also looked to the man who, in turn, studied him with calculating eyes. Kyle gestured to the bandage on his own chest and then pointed to the sprawled figure. Roberts held out another roll of gauze for all of them to see.

Come on! It doesn't get any more obvious than this!

The native seemed to read the unspoken words. The others watch him in dead silence.

Either you let us help him or he is going to die!

The leader gazed with hard eyes at the troopers. The man took one last glance at the bandage before he tossed his hand axe to the ground. With a rough voice he gestured to the others and they slowly lowered their weapons and moved back.

The leader pointed to the fallen man and Doc quickly passed Kyle with his aid bag. The sergeant talked into his helmet microphone while Reeves covered the remaining warriors with his carbine. The sergeant spoke to Kyle with smoldering disapproval.

"Get your shit back on, 'hero'."

Kyle obediently backed over to his gear and got dressed. In a voice loud enough for only the young trooper to hear the sergeant muttered angrily,

"You do something like that again and I'll shoot you myself."

* * *

CHAPTER IV

At the time it had felt like the right thing to do. Once the rush of the moment wore off however, a fear of disciplinary action grew within Kyle. He had already raised the ire of the Lieutenant, and wondered what this latest episode would bring.

Master Sergeant Holly arrived on the scene and the sergeant wasted no time in venting his anger. Failure to obey a direct order and dereliction of duty was the charge. Holly listened quietly as the sergeant spent his steam and then sent the man on his way.

The entire time Kyle, who was working alongside Doc Roberts, was within ear shot of the tirade. As Holly approached, the two were busy strapping another wounded native to a litter. Having completed the task the casualty was carried off. Taking a deep breath, Kyle looked up to the patiently waiting Master Sergeant, unaware of what was to follow.

"Evans."

"Master Sergeant?"

Holly looked at him for a moment before he proceeded.

"I hear you've been busy."

"Yes, Master Sergeant."

Kyle could tell by Holly's there would be no chewing out at that moment. Roberts strolled over as he dug through his kit bag and said to the senior man,

"We're running low on everything. We've got another forty litter cases and the rest will be able to move with a little assistance."

Roberts glanced at Kyle and then back to Holly. The medic seemed to read the situation having overheard the earlier outburst from the sergeant.

"Evans here saved a bunch of lives. If he hadn't done what he did we definitely would have lost a couple right then and there. Probably more if the situation had escalated."

Holly quieted Roberts with a hand gesture and a nod.

"Relax Doc; I'm not going to skin your protégé just yet."

For a moment the three surveyed the scene around them before Holly wandered off to supervise the other aid and litter teams. Roberts flashed a grin to Kyle and punched him playfully in the arm before the two selected their next patient.

For the remainder of the day they transported the seriously wounded into the perimeter for medical attention. Over the next few hours the medics did what they could with what they had to save the lives of their patients. There were a few miracles performed but a good number of the critical cases did not pull through.

The walking wounded were broken down into smaller groups and led into gullies where they could be guarded. At first security was a chief concern, but as time passed so had the apprehension. It appeared the defeated warriors had accepted their lot and no longer resisted. They were far from friendly with their captors but were no longer openly hostile.

A main chieftain was identified and taken to be questioned by the Lieutenant. Those warriors who appeared to be leaders were separated from the others to prevent an uprising. Native weapons were collected and placed in large piles near the armory. Squad shifts were initiated for guard and hospital details.

To the credit of the troopers most of the injuries were leg wounds. There were a few instances of fatal shots to the head and abdomen, most of which were determined to be accidental. A dozen or so of the fatalities were killed when they attacked the security teams. Out of an enemy force of eight hundred and thirty-two only eighteen had died. If the company had played for keeps it was likely that only eighteen would have survived. That was not to say there were no permanent or life altering injuries, but at least the owners were alive to bear them.

Kyle sensed that he had earned Doc Roberts' respect. Despite this admiration, he knew his gamble could have been deleterious. His corpse could be decomposing in a cold, dark grave at that very moment. This point was made very clear by the Lieutenant that evening.

Kyle had stood with heels locked at the position of attention for the last ten minutes. The Lieutenant looked as if he could go on for another hour. The carefully worded reprimand was delivered with aplomb. The commanding officer made it absolutely clear how he felt about Kyle's exercise in judgment.

"…And another thing: The next time you get a harebrained idea like that, you clear it with your chain of command! The reason you have leadership is so that you don't have to do the thinking! Do I make myself absolutely clear!?"

Kyle fought the urge to explain away his actions. Doc Roberts and Master Sergeant Holly already reported what they had witnessed. If their input failed to placate the officer then there was nothing further Kyle could say or do. He unlocked his clenched jaw to speak.

"Yes, sir!"

Conversations in the military often went that way, especially if one was low on the totem pole. It was not the best way to run an operation, but there was no room on the battle field for quibbling.

The Lieutenant appeared to smolder as he searched himself for any remaining fury. Kyle was sure the officer was nearing the end of his rage. Then again, it was an opportune time to unload any residual stress. Instead, the officer picked up a data pad and scanned the contents before he spoke.

"Master Sergeant Holly seems to think that you're not a lost cause. Your progress in remedial instruction is 'exemplary' – his words not mine."

Kyle was surprised by the admission. The Lieutenant continued,

"Your squad leader reports no disciplinary problems, you have no outstanding deficiencies in your readiness report, and short of this stunt you seem to be a qualified and competent trooper."

"Thank you, sir!"

The Lieutenant glared up at him and Kyle wished he could suck the words back into his mouth. He grimaced slightly and blurted,

"I mean….yes, sir!"

The Lieutenant continued to glare at him for a long minute while mulling something over in his head. Satisfied, he straightened and nodded to Holly.

"Very well, Master Sergeant. If you still wish to continue you may proceed."

Holly stepped forward and produced a piece of paper.

"Attention to orders!"

At that, the others present in the office stopped what they were doing and stood at attention. The Lieutenant stepped out from behind his desk as he fumbled with something in his hands.

"The Magistrate of System has reposed special trust and confidence in the patriotism, valor, and fidelity of Private Kyle Edward Evans."

The Lieutenant stood directly in front of Kyle and waited as Holly continued to read. For a second the young trooper was hit with a wave of confusion.

What the hell is this?

"In view of these qualities and his demonstrated potential for increased responsibility, he is, therefore, promoted to the rank of Corporal, with all the responsibilities that it entails, effective immediately."

The Lieutenant secured something to collar of Kyle's uniform.

"By Order of the Commander, for the Secretary of the Army. Signed Michael C. Taylor, First Lieutenant, Echo Company, Fourth of the Twenty-Seventh Infantry Brigade (Light), Commanding."

The Lieutenant then shook Kyle's hand and took a step back.

He doesn't look like a Michael. Wait, what the hell am I thinking about that for?

Kyle instinctively rendered a salute as he had witnessed previously on numerous occasions. The Lieutenant returned the salute and grumbled,

"You do something like this again and I'll shoot you myself."

With that he dismissed the stunned trooper. Kyle turned to go and was congratulated by Holly and the other sergeants. On his way out they each shook his hand, and Kyle found himself standing outside of the office in a state of confusion. He felt the Corporal rank clipped to his collar and assured himself that he had indeed been promoted.

All this time I was afraid of how they were going to punish me.

Kyle started to grin, but was startled by the sergeant on duty.

"Problem, Corporal?"

Kyle blinked and stared at the man.

"No, Sergeant."

The sergeant gestured with his hand toward the door.

"Then you best run along home and check on your men."

Kyle nodded his head absently and quickly exited the room.

* * *

When Kyle arrived back at the squad bay, he found most of the guys stripped to the waist and cleaning their equipment. Some were joking about something and the laughter died as they all turned to regard him. A moment later their eyes fell onto the Corporal rank.

"GET HIM!"

In unison the squad lurched forward overturning the makeshift chairs and table. Kyle managed a single step backward before the tidal wave of bodies crushed him to the ground. His fellows grabbed him by the arms and legs, then hoisted him into the air with a chorus of jeering voices.

Scrub brushes chafed his skin and someone dumped a glop of pine sap onto his chest and head. Others rubbed the sticky mess into his hair and spread it around while the rest painfully pinched and slapped his arms and legs. Kyle tried to wriggle loose but he was pinned tight. He dared not open his mouth against the pain as it was likely someone would smear something unpleasant in it.

With a sudden heave he was dropped unceremoniously onto the planks of the shower stall floor and doused with cold water which was followed by a coating of fine dust. Kyle sputtered and coughed up some liquid which had made its way up his nose while holding his arms protectively over his head.

He was left on the shower room floor with his eyes and skin burning from the scrubbing and tree sap. Kyle propped himself up against the stall and spat a foul taste from his mouth. His arms and legs ached from the rough handling and he was wiped out. Someone stood backlit in the doorway to the shower.

"A buddy of mine said that your name was on a promotion list he saw at headquarters. Figured it would be the least I could do to swing by and save the ass of a new corporal."

Rey tossed a canteen and Kyle, in his utter exhaustion, nearly missed it.

"Drink some of that. It's hooch that the cooks have been brewing out behind the D-Fac. It goes down okay, but afterward burns like hell."

Kyle unscrewed the cap and took a careful swallow. The mixture was sweet like a dessert, but as he took a breath a wave of fire seared down his throat to his stomach. In offering a hand, Rey managed to get smeared with some of the tree sap. This he wiped off on Kyle's sleeve with a grimace.

"Now there's some creative fun. You're lucky though, when I made Corporal they dragged me down to the motor pool and dropped me into each of the catch pits under the vehicle servicing racks."

Rey took the canteen back from Kyle and had another hit, exhaling through clenched teeth. Rey shook his head at the pitiful sight before him.

"You're a real mess, man. Let's go over to the NCO Bunker and see if they have any good suggestions for getting that stuff off you."

Rey then glanced down at the floor of the shower.

"I don't think this place is going to pass morning inspection, do you?"

Kyle stopped and turned to survey the wreckage from his ordeal. He slid past Rey and stood just inside the squad bay and stared at the others. The guys were silent as they worked on equipment, but all grinned impishly. Kyle focused for a moment as he felt the warmth of the alcohol in his blood.

"Calhoun and Buster. Get in here and clean that mess up."

The two troopers jump to their feet and replied in unison.

"Roger that... Corporal!"

The rest continued to work in silence. Rey gestured to Reeves and tossed him the canteen.

"You're in charge until we get back. I'm going to take Evans here down to get a once-over by Doc. Looks like he fell down or something."

Reeves punched the air in a display of success as the others let out a groan of annoyance. The two corporals exited the squad bay into the night. Rey reevaluated the sticky sap that clung to his fingers.

"I think you're going to have to shave that stuff off of you."

As they trudged wearily alongside each other, Kyle gently touched the hardening goop all over his head and let out a half hearted sigh of defeat.

* * *

The hardest part of training a soldier was to communicate what it was that you wanted him to do. Harder still was instructing someone in the art of warfare without the benefit of a common language.

To his surprise Kyle was transferred to an auxiliary unit composed entirely of natives who had volunteered. The Lieutenant and the Chieftain had come to terms with their differences and formed an alliance. The next logical step was to incorporate the warriors into a sister unit which would support future operations. This comingled organization would help to cement mutual trust and dependency.

As the weeks passed more of the warriors were back on their feet and returned to their duties. Those who did not have the responsibility to family or friends elected to stay and serve alongside the new arrivals. As the recruits were assigned to their respective squads, Kyle and the other squad leaders were forced to use a mix of language and hand gestures in order to communicate the most basic of instructions. At first there were a lot of hand movements and sound effects, but the two groups soon learned common key words, and the training began despite a rocky start.

That said, it was far from easy to become responsible for the welfare and performance of a bunch of strangers. Kyle was assigned an area in the nearby pines which was designated as the site of the new squad bay. Several days of non-stop labor and harvested timber yielded a relatively nice home in the ground. In fact, his natives convinced Kyle to modify the build plan in such a way that the end result was a dwelling much larger and stronger than anticipated.

The other area in which the warriors excelled was melee combat and scouting. Kyle led the squad to the nearby grassy field where he indicated he wanted to see their fighting style. The men quickly got into the spirit of the demonstration and several received bleeding cuts and multiple bruises. During the sessions Kyle tried to absorb every detail of their fighting technique so that he could use them on Holly. The natives seemed eager and willing to share what they knew.

The discussion as to whether or not the natives should be trained in the use of the carbines and machineguns was long and heated. The pros and cons were debated for several nights until the Lieutenant decided it was not the right time to teach their new allies how to use the weapons.

However, this did not prevent the men in his squad from asking Kyle questions. He often found that he had to feign confusion when pressed by some of the more observant warriors about the carbines. He could see their frustration trying to learn about the weapons that so easily defeated them during the battle. All of the natives had healed wounds, reminders of the projectiles that had pierced their skin. The 'bite' of the 'slings' that the troopers wielded were respected by those who had experienced it.

The natives were especially proud of their expertise in hunting and foraging. A steady supply of fowl, fish, and mountain goat supplemented the usual venison ration. Wild tubers, onions, and even hearty nuts appeared and the diets of the troopers turned for the better. Kyle forgot how good fresh cheese tasted until one of the natives handed him a small wheel of it during a chow break.

Since the vast majority of the roles the native unit would fulfill were scouting and light fighting, the auxiliaries were often referred to as rangers. In addition, the ranger cadre was now authorized to wear a native fighting knife as part of their official uniform, a gesture meant to further ties between the different peoples.

Most rangers sported several types of hand weapons from small axes to savage fighting blades. Kyle was particularly proud of a bone handled dagger given to him by the Chieftain as a gift for his selfless act after the fight. He felt good to have the warmth and acceptance of the people he led.

Initially it was difficult for Kyle to remember the names of the men in his charge, as they were difficult to pronounce. Each had an assigned roster number but it, too, was cumbersome. Instead Kyle had them merely count off.

The ranger company was made up of two platoons with fifty men broken down into squads of ten. It took the natives a while to figure out what Kyle was trying to do, but soon all had mastered counting to ten in Universal. He lined them up and gave them the order to 'count off'. The rangers counted together in their rough accents as Kyle pointed to each man in turn.

"#Won, Tew, Tree, For, Fife, Seeks, Savan, Ate, Neyen, Ten!#"

The natives grinned like idiots once they finished the count to the last man in line. Kyle then called each number out of sequence and the desired man was trained to step out and bark his assigned number. At first all was well, but later it became apparent that order of precedence for marching had something to do with their numbering.

The ugly moment occurred as the squad was forming to move off for noon chow, when some low grumbling turned into a shoving match. The whole squad was soon at each other's throats and Kyle panicked as a slug fest ensued.

At that precise moment, Master Sergeant Holly appeared and stood silently next to Kyle, who only stared helplessly at his new platoon leader. Holly seemed to take the whole scene in and muttered under his breath,

"Looking good, Evans, looking good. Keep up the good work."

Kyle watched him wander off as the rangers continued to battle for supremacy. They soon picked themselves up from the ground and stumbled into the new marching order.

"#Seeks..., For..., Tew..., Tree..., Fife..., Won..., S'van..., Ten..., Ate..., Neyenh!#"

Kyle stood dumbfounded for a second time in as many moments. The new leader turned and looked at him from the first position. He had a swelled left eye and bloody scrape on his shoulder. Kyle shook himself in to action and quickly marched them off before they had a second chance to revisit the current pecking order.

And I thought it was tough earning my stripes!

The rangers were actually good at marching and had a habit of emitting a deep guttural hum each time their left foot hit the ground. It must have been a necessary part of their training as warriors, and after a while Kyle found that he also started to mimic the technique.

As the weeks continued, a current of warm weather increased the amount of time the squad spent off in the surrounding countryside. Kyle was able to live off the land with a great deal of comfort and minimal use of his issued field equipment. The rangers often snuck a feel of the thermal blanket or tapped their fingernails against his helmet when they thought he would not notice.

Soon Kyle could move nearly as fast and as quietly as his men and the squad began a series of mock raids on an 'enemy' installation. During one particular night mission against a machinegun position, his warriors managed to hang a pair of deer testicles on the barrel of the gun, much to the dismay of the crew who found it there the next morning. Had these warriors been allowed to melt back into the countryside, Kyle could only imagine a guerilla war against such a silent and crafty foe.

After repeated attempts it became obvious that his combat armor prevented Kyle from mastering the skills of his natives, and he soon stowed it whenever the squad went out on exercise. He was forced to bring his helmet however, as it contained his radio as well as other essential features and the inconvenience was worth the added benefit.

Lieutenant Taylor appeared one day on a surprise inspection and discovered Kyle sans armor. The last thing the commander wanted to do was to lose a trooper to a wound that the simple protection would have prevented. Kyle could appreciate the concern, but it was virtually impossible to move silently with the bulky plates and padding. If the squad was well outside the possibility of crossing the Lieutenant, Kyle often went native, much to the approval of his rangers.

As the squad patrols pushed further and further from the shelter of the valley, Kyle began to take more liberty with how he conducted training. The men taught him everything they knew about survival and warfare. Kyle learned everything from locating wild tubers to implementing several techniques with a dagger that would be effective in silencing a sentry. After training with his rangers as a cohort for almost two months Kyle finally resolved what he considered to be a gross error.

On the next long range patrol, Kyle halted the squad in a sheltered valley filled with a thick growth of dense pine. He carefully placed the rangers in a tight perimeter and made it absolutely clear that they were to warn him if anyone approached.

After the disaster of attempting to number his men, Kyle had learned all of his rangers by name. The winner of the contest for seniority was a good natured brute named Taulk. It was him that Kyle led back through the dense pines to a steep embankment of mud and clay. There Kyle halted and un-slung his carbine and to the great surprise of the ranger offered Taulk the weapon.

The native stared at the carbine for a long moment and then looked at Kyle.

"#Rangers no touch slinger.#"

Kyle nodded his head in understanding.

"Yes, I know this is the order of the commander. I don't agree with the commander. I believe that you rangers should be able to know how the weapon works."

Taulk looked at the carbine but made no effort to reach for it. Kyle again offered it to the native but the man backed away slightly.

"Why won't you take it?"

Taulk simply stared at the weapon.

"#Ranger oath no touch slinger.#"

Frigging leadership. They always know better, but it's my ass out here in the wind if things go sour.

Kyle had done his best to put down his irritation. He knew there had to be a loophole in the way a native thought about the situation. Being the only trooper in the squad, it would be of great advantage if his rangers could pick up the carbine and continue the fight. Kyle relaxed his arm and cradled the weapon with his right hand.

"Taulk, do you agree that your life is in my hands when we go to fight?"

Taulk looked at Kyle and tilted his head to the right once. Natives nodded their head to the right for a positive and left for a negative.

"#Yes. Ranger life is in ranger hand.#"

Okay, that's a good angle to exploit.

"So you agree that my life is in your hands when we fight?"

Again Taulk nodded firmly to the right. Thinking carefully Kyle continued.

"If I were to fall in combat don't you think it would be a good idea if you were able to use the carbine to save the rest of the squad - including me?"

Taulk thought on this for a while.

"#But Lieutenant us swear oath.#"

Kyle waved him off.

"The commander had you swear an oath that you would not touch a weapon without our permission. The point he was trying to make is that he did not want you touching our gear without our supervision. I am telling you that it is okay for you to take the weapon."

Again Taulk stared at the carbine but made no move to take it.

"Taulk, I'm giving you a direct order to take the carbine."

Taulk looked at Kyle. He carefully reached out and took the weapon. Holding it, the ranger carefully appraised the item of unspoken value as if he might damage it. Kyle smiled, remembering the first time he held one himself.

It is only a few years ago but feels like an eternity.

"It feels very light but it is stronger than any steel you may know of. Do not be afraid of hurting it as you will not be able to do so."

Kyle showed Taulk how to chamber a projectile and even ejected one so that the native could inspect it more closely. Taulk squeezed and turned the object over in his hand as if memorizing every last detail with his finger tips. It truly seemed a mystery to the ranger how the weapon could force the projectile through a man at such a distance. Kyle had often noted the scar on Taulk's calf where someone had shot him during the brief clash at the pines.

Hell, for all I know it could have been me who did it.

After the initial inspection, Kyle showed Taulk how to load the projectile into the ammo brick before sliding it into the carbine. Then he demonstrated proper position for standing, sitting, and prone firing. Kyle reinforced the penetration and range of the projectile to help the ranger think about when and how to take a shot.

Finally he demonstrated proper sight picture, breathing, and trigger squeeze. After cautioning Taulk about keeping the butt stock tight into the crook of the shoulder, Kyle showed the man how to take the weapon off of safe and what the other settings on the carbine were for. Kyle handed him the carbine again and stepped back, pointing to a large clump of clay.

"Alright Taulk, let's see if you can hit that piece of dirt."

Taulk placed the carbine into his shoulder and wrapped the sling around his forearm as he had been instructed. Kyle watched him take up a sight picture. The native began a deep cleansing breath and held half of it in.

Now we'll see how good of a shot they are!

For several seconds Kyle waited for Taulk to fire but nothing happened. He glanced over at the native and noticed that the man had become so rigid that the carbine trembled in his grasp. Taulk just kept aiming at the large clod of dirt with his finger hovering over the trigger.

Nothing happened.

Holy shit, he's petrified!

After a long, tense moment Kyle spoke.

"Taulk."

The man seemed to relax visibly.

"#Yes, Corporal.#"

"Squeeze the trigger, Taulk."

Nothing.

"#I not, Corporal.#"

What the hell did they threaten to do to these guys?

Kyle slowly stepped toward the ranger. He remained quiet for a long moment, allowing Taulk the opportunity to work up the nerve to pull the trigger. The silence seemed like an eternity.

"Taulk."

The native slumped slightly but the muzzle was still pointed toward the bank of mud.

"Taulk, if you are worried about punishment it is already too late. According to you the oath you took was to never touch one of our weapons and you are already holding one. You're already busted."

Alarmed, Taulk glanced sideways at Kyle, who feigned condolence.

"Your only chance at redemption is that you were obeying my order. If you don't pull the trigger then you are not following my instructions and you're screwed. So you might as well pull the trigger."

The ranger regained his stance and took a sight picture. Once again he blew out half of a deep breath.

And just stood there.

"God damn it Taulk! Pull the fucking trigger!"

CRACK!

The two of them stood for a moment as the sound of the carbine faded from their ears. Taulk was still pointed at the bank of clay; his eyes were wide open. Kyle looked to the target and found the chunk of clay had a large piece blown out of the upper right corner. The real test was not whether Taulk could get an initial bulls-eye but rather if he could keep a tight shot group.

"Alright, that's good, that's good! See? It's wasn't so bad! Now aim for the exact same spot you first fired at and shoot again."

CRACK!

The second shot barely cleaved another small nick out of the clod but it was exactly where it should have been.

"One more time - fire!"

CRACK!

For a long moment they both just stood there. Taulk lowered the carbine and Kyle reminded him to put the weapon back on safe.

"That's real good Taulk, that's real good."

The native had not seemed convinced.

"#I not good slinger.#"

Kyle understood. Even though Taulk had the sights pointed dead center all three projectiles he fired went high and to the right.

"Actually it's really good. The thing that is important is that all three shots hit in the same location. That means you are doing everything correctly, otherwise the shots would be all over the place."

Kyle took the carbine from Taulk and showed him how to adjust the sights. With a few easy clicks he handed the weapon back to the native.

"Okay, shoot at the same exact spot you did last time."

Taulk smoothly took up his stance, aimed, breathed and fired.

CRACK!

The clod of earth exploded with a direct hit. Kyle grinned and glanced at Taulk. The man lowered the weapon while switching it on safe. He stared at the shattered earth then he looked at Kyle.

A huge smile appeared on his face.

"Alright! Send me Neel and check on the others. We've got some rangers to train!"

* * *

CHAPTER V

At first the excitement quieted his anxiety, but time soon forced Kyle to slowly crack under the pressure of his blatant insubordination. It had been three days since he broke Special Order Number One and the sky had still not fallen. Kyle had to force himself to relax and try to breathe a little easier.

It's the "I'll shoot you myself" comments that don't help.

After the last of his rangers completed the basic rifle marksmanship training he brought them together for a brief powwow. He explained why he had issued his own Special Order and taught them how to fire the carbine. Kyle reminded them to keep silent about what they learned and not to use their training unless the situation was life or death. He made it clear what the Lieutenant would do if headquarters caught on.

Kyle had actually thought long and hard about what he was going to do before he took action. It was a calculated risk and perhaps a necessary one to ensure that his men could continue to fight the mission should something happen to him. If the carbine was going to be of use to the rangers as a whole, then the whole of the rangers needed to know how to use it. Besides, it might actually save his life one day.

As far as Kyle was concerned the same went for the other weapons in the company arsenal as well as the tactics. He knew it would be more of a challenge to get the warriors to understand, being men, in principal, from the Iron Age of Earth. That said, their current knowledge of modern equipment was comparable to his own when he had first enlisted so he knew learning was not an impossible task.

After all I've managed to make it this far.

Point of fact, the rangers had been living and fighting the way of true warriors since birth. If anything, they actually had an advanced level of training above him when it came to killing the other guy and winning. The main concern, as far as Kyle saw it, was that trained natives might one day turn the weapons and tactics of the modern age against the company itself.

But that could happen today anyway. Heck I could go nutty and just start shooting up the place. There is no way to guarantee loyalty except through successful integration and dedication.

Kyle could see the rationale behind Special Order Number One until the natives became an integral part of the fighting force. Once that happened, to define a boundary between the two groups was just accentuating a weakness in the organization. In his mind the natives stopped being 'them' and started being 'us' the moment they picked up a weapon to fight for the company as rangers.

We're in this together or not at all.

In the off hours Kyle spent as much time with the rangers as he could. This reinforced bonding within the squad and provided ample opportunity to master each other's language. That night the conversation was an interesting one.

"#You come from the sky?#"

Kyle looked up from his place at the campfire not knowing who had asked the question. He thought on this a moment and cocked his head to the right as he pointed upward.

"Yes. We all came here from the sky."

The rangers exchanged brief looks. Lemm spoke next.

"#How?#"

At this Kyle exhaled slowly while contemplating an answer.

How do I explain this when I don't even know how it works myself?

"There is this thing called a ship. That ship carries smaller ships. Those smaller ships carry me."

Quickly glancing at the rangers, Kyle could see their brains trying to process the notion. Most seemed to fail so he reached over and picked up a small stone which he held up for the others to see.

"Pretend this is me."

He then held up a small pouch from off of his waist belt.

"Pretend this is a small ship."

Kyle dropped the stone into the pouch.

"That's me getting into the small ship."

Kyle took his helmet and held it upside down.

"This is a big ship."

He took the pouch and dropped it into the helmet.

"Now the small ship is inside of the big ship."

Kyle stood up.

"Now pretend that the big ship can think about standing over on the opposite side of the fire. Poof!"

He hopped over to the other side.

"Instantly it is there. So I got into a small ship which was loaded into a big ship and the big ship thought about being here and *poof* we arrived. The small ship then carried us down to the surface."

The rangers turned and talked to each other in low tones. Although Kyle had become semi-proficient in their tongue he could not make out what was said as they talked over each other. Lemm seemed confused.

"#How?#"

Kyle let out a slight laugh at this.

"To be honest I don't entirely know myself. I'm a soldier and I go where I am told. I don't necessarily know how things work, but I know that they do certain things and so I learn how to use them. Like this."

With that Kyle held up the carbine for them to see.

"I know that there is something inside here that takes the air and forces the projectile out the barrel, but how it really works or even what it is made of is beyond my current understanding."

Taulk nodded and spoke.

"#It is like healing arts. Not all truly understand but salves on wound heal better.#"

Kyle cocked his head right in acknowledgement and smiled at Taulk.

"Exactly."

The warrior seemed pleased with this and enjoyed his new role as sage.

"#Do you come from the Darkness?#"

Kyle did not know what to make of the question.

"Darkness? I don't know what you mean."

One of the rangers pointed up to the night sky. Kyle glanced up but he had no idea what they were talking about. Taulk, once again, came to the rescue.

"#It is said the night sky is a dark blanket placed there by the Spirits. To help us see in the night the Spirits have scattered precious stones across the blanket which shine their light down upon us. The Darkness is something that moves across the sky hiding the light of the stones. This is the only way that we know of the Darkness or where it is in the sky.#"

The rangers stared at Kyle and studied his face as he absorbed the lore.

Sounds logical to me if I were them.

Taulk turned and studied the ridge of the mountain behind them. After a few moments he pointed up to the peak.

"#Do you see the light that shines a hand width above the top of the mountain?#"

Kyle moved past the fire to place the light of the flames behind him. Standing beside Taulk he allowed his eyes to adjust to the night and quickly located the star in question.

"#Watch it now.#"

The group sat in dead silence as they waited. Although Kyle could not see their faces he knew that they, too, cast a fixed gaze on the twinkling light in question. He had no idea what was about to happen. Taulk suddenly pointed again and Kyle looked up his arm as a guide.

"#There!#"

As he watched, the bright star began to twinkle differently; the light suddenly became drunk and unstable. A second later it made a small arc and winked out of existence. Silent awe and fear descended over the rangers. Several turned away and made protective wards with their hands. In puzzled silence Kyle turned to Taulk.

"What is it?"

Taulk and the rangers continued to watch the spot in the sky without speaking so Kyle returned to the vigil. Several seconds later the shimmering star mysteriously reappeared in the night sky.

Kyle turned and looked at the other rangers, who merely poked at the fire with small sticks. Again he turned to Taulk.

"What is it?"

After a moment Taulk replied, although he still looked at the stars.

"#There many different people in our lands and they all have different beliefs. To most the Darkness is an evil spirit that roams the night sky and brings bad luck or death. These people say the Darkness steals or eats the lights in the night. Others think of the Darkness as a thief which moves stealthily. These people say that the Darkness borrows the light or that the lights dim in a show of respect as the Darkness passes.#"

Evil spirit or sneaky thief. I'm going with the latter.

Kyle turned back to try and guess the path of the object as it traveled overhead. For it to block the light of a distant star meant it was closer to the planet. To move across the light so quickly meant that it had to be in orbit. Perhaps it was a dark moon or a captured asteroid. Since it did not reflect the light from the nearby star it must be dark in color. Kyle stood next to Taulk who continued to watch the night sky.

"What do you think it is?"

Taulk almost seemed amused by the question.

"#Many things I not know. This one more. I not fear Darkness but I careful of worshipers of evil spirit.#"

The man turned and looked at Kyle in such a way that the warning was not lost.

"Who worships the Darkness as evil?"

Taulk turned back to the sky.

"#Not here, at least not openly…forbidden. Mostly great plain to the sun rise.#"

East. He means to the east. From the look he gave me I don't want to find out what these people do.

Kyle turned back to the rangers, who stared at him. He realized that he had not answered their original question.

"Oh! No, no, no. I'm not from the Darkness. I come from a place very far away. In fact those lights you see in the sky are actually stars like the sun which brings the daylight. My land is located near one of those suns."

From the blank look on their faces Kyle could tell that he just lost them all, however they also seem relieved. Lemm seemed to be the only one interested in pressing for more detail.

"#Which one?#"

Kyle slumped at this. He looked to the sky to scan the unfamiliar cascade of stars and felt a helplessness come over him. He spoke in a subdued voice.

"I honestly have no idea."

The men all remained silent and returned their attention to the embers glowing in the fire. Taulk pointed again and Kyle watched another star wink out of existence. Moments later it reappeared.

It moves in a straight line and it is definitely in orbit of this planet.

A sneaking fear was suddenly upon him.

What if it's not natural? We could be in danger! I have to tell Holly about this!

Turning back to Lemm Kyle asked,

"Why did you want to know if I 'come from' the Darkness? Do you know of people who have?"

Taulk stopped following the track of the invisible moon and looked at Kyle.

"#There always lights in sky long my people remember. Darkness discovered generations past. Ten seasons ago Darkness flashed light and sky filled fiery rain for days after.#"

Kyle looked up and picked out the elusive target again. Taulk continued to talk.

"#It said where fire struck ground powerful tribe walked land. Worshipers raid not long after as a sign of new master to kill weak. Many years I heard stories as child and treated them such until our clan raid great plain to free our people.#"

"#Nomads became Horde, rise to power, no peace for people. Clansmen sacrificed to new master, The One, Child of the Darkness. Rumors of others, but scattered.#"

Kyle stood in shocked silence trying to absorb it all as he processed the information.

We're not alone. Whoever they are they came from that thing in orbit and they have been here for years already.

Kyle kept his composure in front of the others.

They don't need to see me wig out over some children's story.

He wondered who these people might be and why they scattered themselves across the planet to remain in seclusion. Kyle knew that the war he volunteered for had been going on for the last three years, or so, and figured it had nothing to do with that.

"#We get to see dragon?#"

Kyle turned back to the fire pit and looked at Neel who spoke.

"Dragons?"

Kyle glanced at Taulk and then back to Neel, gesturing for him to continue.

"#Yes, Corporal, dragons you ride in sky.#"

Kyle noticed that all faces were on him again.

This must be of interest to all of them.

"I'm sorry Neel, I don't know what you're talking about. Can you describe the 'dragons' to me?"

The young man appeared to study Kyle's face as if to detect deception but, finding none, continued.

"#Before your people in valley many tales of dragons.#"

Kyle thought on this.

Does he mean the drop ships?

"Describe them to me."

Neel appeared unsure.

"#Grandfather told me dragons very large. Bigger than central hut of village. Great beast roar when fly and eat whole flock sheep one sitting.#"

Kyle was perplexed.

The dragons he speaks of were here long before we were.

Neel continued,

"#After night you come many our hunters see if more Children Darkness. They follow dragons up valley, found you.#"

To Kyle it sounded like sightings of the drop ships.

They must have our transports confused with their beasts.

Kyle had no idea how big a central hut was, but it sounded as though the young warrior was describing the drop ships flying up and down the valley. He thought carefully for a moment before replying.

"Yes. I do not think they are the same dragons that your grandfather spoke of, but we do have something like this…."

Reaching down Kyle took a small bundle of sticks and tossed it onto the glowing embers. With a slight breath the flames sprang up and all could see quite clearly. He then took a small piece of charcoal and drew on the large rock which made up the backstop to the fire. When Kyle finished and shifted back the rangers moved closer for a better view.

"I think our drop ships are the recent dragon sightings you speak of."

The rangers all seemed excited as they quietly talked amongst themselves. Kyle had to smile himself at their childlike energy.

I remember the first time I saw a plane flying overhead.

Kyle knew that the natives had never seen a thing as large as a drop ship flying in the sky. Only creatures from their lore could come close to a fair comparison. Now they were part of an army that actually flew with such things. Lemm smiled a wide grin and looked to Kyle.

"#So it true? You fly them?#"

Kyle sat back and thought for a moment.

"Well, we control them but they are not the same dragons your grandfather spoke of. These are more like flying huts that carry us to where we want to go."

The rangers again muttered amongst themselves.

"#You fly in them?#"

Kyle had not known who asked the question, but tilted his head to the right in affirmation.

"If I have my way, someday you will too."

Looks of apprehension appeared on their faces except for Lemm who seemed thrilled beyond belief. Kyle remembered their first time with the carbine.

Getting these guys to climb into the gut of something that screams on landing is not going to be easy.

Kyle spent the rest of the night trying to acclimate his men as best he could to the modern equipment they would be exposed to. The conversation was semi productive and went on long into the night. Kyle found that the best way to get around the technical understanding was to simply refer to certain functions as magic; in a way it was.

When the patrol returned back to the company area Kyle decided to talk to Holly about the discussions. He stepped up to the doorway and knocked twice on the frame.

"Master Sergeant, can I have a word with you?"

Holly looked up from some papers on his makeshift desk and gestured for Kyle to sit down.

"What's on your mind Evans?"

Kyle stared absently at the papers which Holly stacked neatly into a pile before placing them aside.

"The natives know about the drop ships."

Holly only looked at him.

"We were out on a training exercise past the western ridge and I had set up a patrol base for the night. During the course of the conversation they started asking me about dragons."

Holly leaned back against the wall of his bunker and mused.

"Dragons."

"Yes, Master Sergeant. That's how they described it to me at least. It seemed very similar to the same stories I grew up with about great flying monsters. I asked them to describe what they were talking about and it appears that a hunting party witnessed our landing in the valley, and associated our drop ships with their beasts from lore. That's why Rey and I ran into that guy who jumped me. He was part of a group sent to scout for the dragons and was probably scared out of his wits."

Holly thought on it.

"What did you tell them?"

Kyle recalled the conversation from the previous evening.

Maybe he thinks I shouldn't have told them anything. That never occurred to me.

"Well, I didn't deny it. I just told them that we have flying huts that take us where we want to go, and that I thought it was these which they had mistaken for their monsters."

Holly sighed.

"Yeah, 'how do you explain to someone about rock and roll'?"

Kyle looked at the man, slightly confused. Holly laughed to himself and got up from the desk to stretch. He walked over to a large map mounted on the wall and momentarily stared at it.

"They seem pretty sure these dragons belong to us? It isn't something else that we don't know about?"

The question struck Kyle as a bit odd but he thought it over.

"Well, they have their own stories that seem pretty old in origin, but I think that what they saw in the sky, most recently was our drop ships, Master Sergeant. Otherwise, I think either we, or the pilots, would have seen or heard something by now."

Holly looked at the map. After a long moment he sighed again.

"Well, they saw what they saw and they know what they know. Let them chew on that for a bit but don't tell them any thing more. You have anything else for me?"

Kyle nodded his head.

"They wanted to know if we were 'Children of the Darkness'."

At this, Holly turned and looked at him intently. Kyle related the whole story as best he could recall, as explained by Taulk. The senior man moved slowly back to his chair as he listened in silence. When Kyle finished, Holly sat back and rested his hands across his stomach. After reflecting he spoke.

"Evans, one of the biggest challenges you will have to face as a leader is the all feared rumor mill. I'm going to tell you something that doesn't leave this room. Understand?"

Kyle nodded his head.

Holly leaned forward and spread his hands out on the desk in front of him as he continued.

"The Chieftain told us of a people who came from the sky about ten years ago. As best we can tell there was some sort of station or observation platform orbiting this planet and something went wrong. The crew abandoned ship and most made it through the rain of debris to the surface in escape pods."

Kyle sat in stunned silence.

They already knew all of this!

He fought down the surge of anger that boiled up inside of him.

Am I just pissed that they can keep a secret and I can't?

Holly continued,

"As best we can tell, some have mixed with local populations and started influencing things. Others have barricaded themselves into seclusion. Either way we have no idea who they are or where they're from. Most importantly we don't know if they're friendly or if they'll want us dead."

Kyle thought about the Horde and their evil worship of the Darkness.

I wonder who this dreaded 'One' really is.

"So we've pushed out our aerial recon and foot patrols, making wider and wider sweeps to identify any sign of the survivors. In the meantime we've yet to hear a peep from the *Rosalie* or Fleet. Furthermore, the best friends we have planet side are a bunch of people we had to shoot in the ass in order for them to throw in with us."

Kyle nodded his head absently as he listened.

"For the time being the Lieutenant has ordered that this be kept to a 'need to know' basis. Since you found out on your own I want you to know what we know. This way you can keep the bullshit from circulating, and an ear out for other bits of the picture that might be of use to us. I entrust you to keep a tight lip on this, as the last thing we need is for our people to start getting spooked by the unknown. The mind of a trooper has a tendency to wander in the worst case direction."

Kyle nodded as he remembered his own experiences.

"Did you have anything else for me?"

Kyle thought briefly to come clean with Holly and tell him about training his rangers to fire the carbine. After a serious second thought he recanted.

"No, Master Sergeant."

* * *

Later that evening the Lieutenant called a briefing for the cadre of the ranger company. The commander had decided that it was in the best interest of the unit to tell their native cohorts as little as possible about themselves. The officer acknowledged that some may disagree with the policy but he felt that the troopers needed to focus on getting information and not on giving it. During the briefing Kyle watched Holly and noted the strictly neutral mask the senior man maintained.

That means he doesn't agree with the Lieutenant.

Knowing this brought Kyle some relief. If word got out about his training the natives, maybe Kyle would have half a chance if his platoon leader was of the same mindset.

Then again maybe he'll 'shoot me himself'.

A few weeks later a small party of warriors made contact with one of the local security patrols. The patrol leader radioed in to file a report on the company frequency. Kyle and a number of others had tuned their helmets to the same, thus being privy to the intelligence. What they all heard was brief and ominous.

Word of the company's arrival, the return of legendary 'dragons' had spread like wildfire. Far to the east the marauding Horde took a sudden interest in the news, and roving bands began to move west across the great steppe. The One had announced a decree of reward to any who captured the new arrivals - and death to those who harbored them.

The Chieftain and his people were unfazed, as the Horde had actively tried to subjugate them before without success. After a detailed review of existing aerial reconnaissance, and other intelligence collected by the local patrols, Lieutenant Taylor decided to send out several long range recons. These were to gather more detailed information from the ground in regards to the avenues of approach into the valley.

Kyle and his rangers were ordered by Holly to trace a winding path and locate critical points, as well as search for evidence of Children along the way. The squad was to be supervised by a senior man from headquarters and came in the form of one Staff Sergeant Melvin Miles Percy.

Percy was an interesting individual who fancied himself as 'in the know' and liked to treat his peers and lower rankers as lesser beings. The sergeant supposedly had a glowing career as a paper pusher, but Kyle had also witnessed enough of his uppity attitude that it left a foul taste in his mouth. Rumor had it that the man bucked for a platoon leader slot and looked to score brownie points by leading a patrol.

From what Kyle gleaned from Holly, if Percy did well it would indeed be a solid step toward a leadership slot. If he did poorly then it was back to the desk job, which the man seemed to disdain. Either way, Kyle was not thrilled about his rangers being used as an acid test for promotion, especially since the situation had become serious.

As Kyle and his rangers packed their gear and performed combat inspections, Percy arrived at the squad bay. He stood in the doorway with his hands on his hips and waited to be noticed. Kyle did not see him at first as he was locked in conversation with Taulk near the back of the room. When he finally did notice the man, it took a moment for Kyle to make his way over.

"Evening, Sergeant."

Percy glared at him for a moment with disapproving eyes.

"So, we don't acknowledge when a senior sergeant enters the room anymore?"

Kyle stared at the man for a moment and realized that he was being serious.

You have got to be kidding me.

Kyle went to the position of attention and called out in a loud and thunderous voice.

"At EASE!"

The rangers all stopped and looked slightly confused as they were not used to the formality. Taulk sensed the mood of the situation and gestured with his hands to the others who quickly stood at attention.

Percy glared down the length of the bay and then back at Kyle.

"I see we have a little work to do with these men, Corporal. They're standing at attention and not at parade rest!"

Oh, for the love of Mary. What is this guy's problem!?

It took every ounce of self discipline for Kyle to not roll his eyes. Holly had long ago done away with the formalities of garrison life subsequent to his numerous visits to the squad areas. Apparently Percy still felt the need to shove his rank into the faces of others.

"Squad! Parade – rest!"

The rangers snapped to the correct position.

Percy nodded his head and smiled thinly.

"Better."

Whatever.

The blank face Kyle wore betrayed none of his thoughts. Percy began to stroll around the squad bay fingering the odd piece of equipment or looking disdainfully at the rough outfit of a ranger. To their credit the men did not stir.

"I shall be responsible for this reconnaissance mission through the northeast corridor. Our goal is to identify any avenues the enemy might exploit against us and to locate any evidence of useful technology or allies. Corporal Evans will be my assistant and second in command. There will be no mistakes and we will perform in such a manner that brings credit to us and our unit."

Kyle felt his neck began to burn.

This guy has been reading too many promotion orders.

Percy stopped his meandering and snapped at the rangers in the bay.

"Do I make myself clear?!"

"YES, SERGEANT!!"

The rangers bellowed in a deafening voice that startled the unsuspecting man. Kyle smiled ever so slightly. The new recruits had mastered Universal at an impressive pace and now had only the barest trace of their native accent when they spoke.

Great, you're afraid of your own men.

Percy quickly regained his composure and strode slowly back to Kyle before standing directly in his face.

"Another thing, Corporal, I am a *Staff* Sergeant and I expect to be acknowledged as such. The next man that addresses me as just a 'sergeant' gets latrine detail for the week. Is that understood!?"

Kyle sounded off into the man's face.

"Yes, *Staff* Sergeant!"

Percy pulled away slightly but appeared satisfied.

"Good. We hit the line of departure tomorrow at 0400 hours. Squad, Atten-tion!"

The rangers snapped to.

"Corporal, take charge of the men and finish preparing for the mission."

Percy then waited in front of Kyle until it dawned on the younger man what was expected of him.

Oh my god, you have got to be kidding me! Where does this clown think he is, at a military academy?

Kyle threw a crisp salute which Percy returned before departing with an air of self importance. Amazed, Kyle could only watch the man disappear down the trench line. At a wave of his arm the others returned to their work, slightly mystified at the whole proceeding. Taulk came over and stood next to Kyle as Percy disappeared.

"This *Staff* Sergeant Percy…"

Kyle turned and looked at the native noting the emphasis.

"…he is an *asshole*, yes?"

Kyle snorted a laugh and shushed Taulk. Heaven help them if Percy had heard that. An old trick of sergeants was to listen in on the room they just left in order to see who the troublemakers were. Soldiers had a tendency to blow off steam right after getting a good grilling when they thought it safe to do so.

Kyle quietly returned to inspecting his rangers and their equipment. It was clear that they had their hands full with Percy. Kyle was already too busy to worry as he conducted rehearsals and reviewed the patrol route with Taulk. After a few more long hours the squad hit the sack for the night.

The next morning the men filtered out of the perimeter at exactly 0400 hours and were counted out by Holly. Taulk took point and led the patrol into a thick growth of pines to the southwest and parallel to the main stream.

Percy suddenly grabbed Kyle by the strap of his combat armor and nearly yanked him off balance. The man hissed into Kyle's ear much too loudly,

"We're going the wrong way, for fuck's sake! Can't you people do anything right?"

Kyle gritted his teeth and bit back his anger. He leaned forward and spoke in a low voice, barely audible.

"Staff Sergeant, it's SOP to depart the patrol base in a direction other than the intended route of travel to throw off anyone who might be observing our departure. Taulk will turn to a northeast heading after he travels a distance of approximately one kilometer. If you watch for it you will get the signal as it is passed down the line."

As understanding dawned on the sergeant, Kyle basically ripped himself free of the grasp and hurried to close the gap created in the patrol column. Percy rushed up from behind and for a second time hissed loudly,

"But he has no compass! How will he know which way to go?"

Burning with irritation Kyle pointed to the dull glow over the horizon.

"The sun, Staff Sergeant, he'll use the sun. The rangers have used the heavens to show them the way for as far back as they can remember. It's also a standard rifleman skill."

After reaching the predetermined distance, Taulk passed back the hand and arm signal for change of direction and proceeded to the northeast. Percy appeared to make no effort to acknowledge the prediction. The rest of the day the squad made its way through the foot of the mountains, slowly winding along the assigned route.

Taulk and another ranger had traveled this course previously and served as guides. They picked the best parallel paths which offered the most concealment and protection to the patrol. Kyle explained to Percy that the column could not use the same path when they returned after the sergeant had failed to comprehend the indirect nature of the route selection. The senior man was correct in that the way traced by Taulk would be much slower, but it also demonstrated his total lack of understanding in regards to patrol tactics.

I hope I never have to serve under this joker again. One day he is going to get a bunch of good people killed.

As they advanced, the walls of the gullies became steeper and the patrol was forced to follow the more obvious ground. Terrain of this kind made Kyle extremely nervous as there was no other choice but to walk through it. He pulled out his photo generated map and noted the location as a choke point. Anyone who approached the valley from the northeast would have to pass through the area.

Per Standard Operating Procedure Kyle pushed the two rangers out further to the front to serve as an advanced warning. The men cleared obvious ambush locations and checked for signs of recent foot traffic. Percy eventually noticed one of the point men and sprinted up to Kyle unable to conceal his excitement. The other rangers in the column turned to see who was making all the noise and glared in disapproval.

It took a few moments but Kyle patiently explained to Percy that the individual he saw was one of their own men. Percy began to argue the point until Taulk reappeared to signal the all clear. The sergeant appeared miffed rather than embarrassed and made some cutting comment about not being kept 'in the loop'. Kyle glared at the man as he strode off down the valley.

Try picking up the Infantry Field Manual and reading it once in a while!

The squad continued to push eastward and the rocky hillsides began to give way to dense packs of tall spindly conifers. The squad moved expertly except for Percy who had a tendency of standing out against the landscape or scuffing his feet. Lemm watched yet another stone skitter across a rocky clearing and glanced at Kyle, who only shrugged his shoulders in helplessness.

What's a Corporal to do?

An essential element of a successful reconnaissance was silence. With this in mind, most infantry developed hand and arm signals to help communicate brief commands or instructions to avoid uttering a word. As the squad became more proficient they could advance the skill to a point where entire conversations were held with just the motion of fingers, hands, and arms. This was also a useful technique to bridge the language barrier.

Percy was too new to the squad to know any of the more advanced signals, but he had not bothered to learn any of the most basic signs either. The result was a man hissing or barking commands to people across a distance that could easily be detected by an enemy in the area. Worse was the fact that the sergeant would not understand a signal which required immediate action thereby jeopardizing the entire mission.

With this in mind Kyle tried to speak to Percy later that night while the patrol was in a temporary base. He had thought long and hard about the best way to approach the senior man so as not to put the sergeant on the defensive. Despite his best efforts the Percy could not be anything but offended.

"Are you *kidding* me?!"

Kyle flinched at the outburst. Glancing at the rangers in the shadows of the pines around them, he could tell they were agitated at the lack of noise discipline.

We're not in friendly territory anymore and these guys are going to stuff him into a tree trunk somewhere if he doesn't pipe down!

Kyle made an obvious effort to speak in a voice that was barely audible despite his close proximity to Percy.

"Staff Sergeant, I mean no offense. It's just..."

Percy seemed to take the lowered tone from Kyle as an admission of guilt. The staff sergeant let fly a tirade that was most likely heard by the security post outside the perimeter.

"Listen here Corporal *Know-It-All*, I've been in this man's Army for over fifteen years without having to do hand puppets or half of that other native voodoo nonsense that you call training."

Nonsense? Since when is basic sound, light, and camouflage discipline nonsense?

"You just remember one thing, and that's *I'm* in charge of this operation not you. If I think it's okay to strut naked down to the stream then that's what is going to happen. We go where I say, when I say, and how I say. In fact, tomorrow, you're relieved of handling the squad. I don't need you interfering with my operation. You just tag along behind me with your mouth shut and your ears open. When I need you to fetch me something I'll let you know. You got me?"

Kyle was stunned at the complete lack of professionalism.

Where did you come from?

"Are you deaf? I asked you a question, *Corporal.*"

"Yes, *Staff* Sergeant."

Satisfied with his successful coup, Percy sat back against his combat pack under a low hanging pine branch.

"Excellent. Now how about you get out on the perimeter security where I don't have to look at your face. This way you can actually do some work for once instead of just walking around like you're hot shit."

Kyle should have felt anger at the rough handling but instead was overcome with a wave of apprehension. The idea of the irresponsible and unskilled man maneuvering his rangers struck him profoundly.

This asshole is going to get my men killed.

He felt it as sure as he knew the sun was going to rise the next day. Numb with the revelation, Kyle secured his gear and crawled out to the perimeter where a ranger marked the passage point that led out of their temporary patrol base. Crawling past the native, Kyle ignored the signed question that was asked and crept up to join Taulk and Rahn in a well camouflaged security position.

Rahn, too, inquired, but Kyle waved him off and signaled for the younger ranger to return to the perimeter to get some sleep. Rahn glanced at Taulk but obeyed, allowing Kyle to crawl into the vacated spot. Next to him the senior ranger glanced over inquisitively, but said nothing.

Kyle signed to the man that Percy was now running the squad. Taulk signed an epithet and surveyed the night around them. Kyle indicated that the two of them had to continue to manage the patrol behind the sergeant's back or he might get them all killed. Taulk acknowledged and gave Kyle the much needed reassurance that things would work out.

On the morning of the fifth day, the patrol left the mountain gullies and entered a chain of foot hills on the eastern mountain slope that led to the passage. Ahead Kyle could see long open valleys covered with old growth trees and open patches of wild grass. To the northeast the mountain chain continued as far as the eye could see and, in the distance, a flat blue green plain of the great steppe appeared to the east. A warm, welcoming breeze blew up from the valley and Kyle found it one of the most welcoming experiences he had had since the company made landfall.

Percy selected a route to the lip of a ridge which would afford an excellent view of the valley approaches below. The only issue Kyle had was that the course led through an area which would leave the patrol exposed and blind to oncoming threats.

Having been banished to the rear of the column, Kyle signaled for the point men to move around the left flank of the danger area. The rangers started to veer off toward the sparse cover when Percy suddenly yelled to them.

Son of bitch! What is that guy doing?!

The sergeant was chastising the rangers so loudly that Kyle could hear most of the reprimand from where he stood.

That's fucking it! They can court-marshal me all they want when we get back but I'll be damned if I'm going to let this mother fucker get away with this!

Furiously, Kyle stormed toward the unsuspecting sergeant who was angrily instructing the point men to proceed through the open ground.

"You people might want to learn some Universal! You know you're in the damned Army now don't you?!"

Kyle closed the distance to the man, trying to decide whether to bust him in the jaw or simply butt stroke him to the head. Suddenly, Taulk signaled a warning from a small ledge on the left flank, where he was providing early warning for the patrol as it prepared to enter the depression.

Danger Close - Enemy - That Way - Closing - Disperse - Hide!

On pure instinct the rangers echoed the signal and instantly melted into the surrounding terrain. Completely oblivious to the warning Percy was shocked by their sudden disappearance.

"Hey! Where the hell do you think you're all going?!"

Kyle forced himself to stay put instead of hiding so that Percy had a chance to see him signaling. The staff sergeant had worked himself into a full rage and spun around seething.

"Evans! What the fuck is going on here!? I told you I'm in charge now you son of a bitch! I'll have your balls for this you insubordinate…!"

The sergeant continued to rage at Kyle and pointed an accusatory finger in his direction. Glancing up and behind the man, Kyle saw a dust cloud waft up from beyond the ridge. Figuring noise discipline was blown anyway, he pointed and called out a warning.

"Watch out! Behind you! Hide!"

The sergeant stopped mid sentence in shock.

"I'm talking now! You shut your filthy hole and listen when you're being spoken to by a superior! This is a one way street you...!"

Kyle stared at the man in disbelief and glanced up again at the dust. Too far away to even think about trying to knock the man down, Kyle dove into a small bunch of pines nearby. Percy was again stunned into silence before exploding in another burst of outrage.

"Insubordination! Insubordination! This is blatant insubordination! I'll have you busted back to Private so fast you'll be shoveling shit with a spoon before you know..."

The anger on Percy's face vanished as he heard a group of cavalry riding up over the small rise behind him. Caught completely by surprise the sergeant turned to face the sound to his rear.

Two dozen men mounted on large dog-like beasts came to a halt on top of the small rise. They wore a combination of black plate and studded armor decorated with long strips of red cloth and hair streaming from the upper arms and helmet. In their arms they carried a wicked assortment of spears and small shields emblazoned with the image of a red eye on a black field.

The mounts appeared to be a crossbreed of huge wolf and short haired dog. Their bodies were covered in a hodgepodge of barding plates, and on their backs were saddles which bore their riders. Huge maws were left bare and displayed rows of long fanged teeth several inches in length. If these were not outriders of the famed Horde then nothing would be. Kyle looked at the motley collection of raiders.

Holy... fucking... shit...!

The riders all looked at Percy who stood in utter bovine incomprehension. The light dust kicked up by the enemy was gently carried away by a soft breeze. From where Kyle hid, it appeared that these men were the sole immediate threat to be dealt with.

A huge man in the middle of the enemy formation pointed with a long, reverse-curved sword which caught the light of the sun. He barked a single command and the riders around him kicked their mounts into action with a deep battle cry. Kyle dropped his eyes to look at Percy.

The wall of bared fangs and charging riders shocked the staff sergeant out of his daze. The raw look of terror on his face explained why the man had not swung up his carbine to fire. Percy ran away from his pursuers and made a straight line for where he had last seen Kyle standing.

He'll never make it.

Kyle felt his stomach as it cinched into a tight knot. He brought his carbine up to his shoulder and assumed a good firing position. The lead attacker leveled his spear and aimed it, as if intent on impaling the fleeing Percy. Without thought, Kyle took a sight picture on the rider, let out half a breath, and squeezed the trigger so smoothly that the carbine surprised him when it fired.

CRACK!

The raider tumbled out of the saddle and drove his mount into the ground with a spray of dust. The other riders maneuvered their dogs slightly so as to avoid becoming entangled with the fallen man. The group continued to close ground on Percy, and Kyle was forced to a half stance in order to acquire the next rider. As he emerged from the pines the attackers, catching sight of him, suddenly reared up and halted their charge. Kyle froze his trigger squeeze mid pull.

Maybe this can end here.

The riders turned and looked back at the leader on the ridge. The man regarded Kyle and assessed the situation. Seemingly convinced that his men could handle this new development, he again pointed his curved sword and bellowed. The riders turned as one and took up their charge once more.

Okay pal, that's going to cost you!

Kyle switched over to target the leader backlit against the sky. As he squeezed off the shot, Percy plowed into him and the two tumbled down a sandy embankment below the knot of pines. Coming to a rest at the bottom of the three meter bank, Kyle struggled to get his footing and spit the grit from his mouth.

"Sergeant Percy! Where the hell are you going!?"

Percy continued his mad scramble and raced toward another line of small trees further away. Kyle listened for the direction from which the raiders would attack and recovered his carbine.

Stay focused or you're going to die!

The cries of the riders faded and a menacing bark of the dogs could be heard instead. It was difficult to determine the direction from which the animals approached due to their soft pads. Their footfalls and jingle of equipment were ambiguous at best.

Pressing his back into the pine trees Kyle nestled close to achieve some rear and flank protection. Moreover, it was unlikely that a mounted attacker would navigate the steep drop he had just tumbled down.

Coming full speed, the first dog rounded the corner from the left with his rider low in the saddle. The massive paws of the animal pounded the ground as Kyle met the eyes of his attacker. The man tightened his crouch and expertly set the long shaft of the spear to drive it through Kyle's heart.

So this is what it looks like when someone wants you dead.

Kyle, in turn, leveled the carbine and squeezed off two quick shots. The rider lifted up and flopped backward across the saddle, but the dog continued, intent on making it to his target.

I hope to god I can stop you before you reach me!

Kyle flipped the selector switch to burst and aimed between the angry eyes that craved for his death. A short rap rocked out of the carbine and the animal landed in a heap of flying sand and pebbles. Kyle had only seconds to collect his wits as more riders appeared on the heels of the first.

Luckily the next two were at a further distance, thus giving Kyle time to aim. Bracing against his tree, Kyle shot the lead man out of the saddle with a short burst, having forgotten to reset the selector lever to semiautomatic. The second man veered his dog further to the outside, thinking a wider pass was safe. Unaware of the capability of a carbine the rider paid for this mistake with his life.

The unguided dogs traveled only a brief distance and seemed confused by the lack of control from a master, who were now unwittingly dragged behind them. Vicious growls were flashed at Kyle as the animals continued to nervously pass him by before loping off to regroup near distant trees. Kyle watched the bodies of the riders trail them unceremoniously across the rough terrain.

Now that's gotta suck.

A general roar of fighting rang out in front of the pines hiding him. Kyle realized that the rangers had ambushed the riders after they saw him disappear. Kyle turned and looked toward the direction in which Percy had fled and was furious to see no trace of the man. It was clear that the sergeant had no backbone for a fight.

And they wouldn't give a carbine to a native!

Fuming, Kyle pushed himself to his feet and advanced in the direction of his last attack. Carbine at the ready, he moved quickly in the loose sand, skirting the small pines toward the sound of fierce shouting and growling dogs.

Climbing the small embankment the scene presented to him was a whirlwind of animals and men locked in a desperate melee. A thick cloud of dust hung thick in the air, shrouding all with a golden curtain of sunlight. It would have been impossible to tell who was who except for the notably high perch of the raiders which clearly indicated them as enemy. Kyle hoped none of his men had made it into a saddle.

Leveling the carbine Kyle blew out two calming breaths before systematically shooting riders from their mounts. The need to quickly drop as many of the enemy as possible was critical as it would be impossible to identify friend if their foe were to dismount.

Fallen enemy were dispatched by shadows which Kyle assumed were rangers. The crazed dogs continued to bark and snarl, flashing their deadly teeth. These animals did not run from close-in fighting as the others had. One of the beasts bristled at a man in front of it and Kyle fired two shots into the head of the rabid monster, effectively ending the contest.

The creature yelped and snapped its massive jaws reflexively as it fell in a convulsing heap. At first Kyle was relieved to have stopped the dog, but he felt guilt on hearing the animal's whimper of pain. Then again, no matter how innocent the creature might be, it still could kill with an easy snap of its deadly teeth. This would be more than enough to give Kyle nightmares for years to come.

Nearly all of the riders and a few of their dogs were down on his side of the dust up. A few twitching bodies and one raider trying to crawl away under his own power was all Kyle could see. He stepped through the twist of fallen bodies and over the still form of a ranger coated in blood and grime. Kyle had no time to notice who it was, but guessed by the size that it was not Taulk.

Several riders broke away from the melee and kicked their dogs toward the small rise from which they had come. Kyle figured if they got away a larger enemy force would be after them in less than an hour. Even as he began to fire he realized with a sense of dread that he could not get them all.

The massive stride of the dogs carried their riders further away with each second that passed, while Kyle emptied his carbine with some of the sloppiest shooting he had ever done. He tried to collect himself as he fumbled for another brick to load into the weapon.

God damn it Evans! Concentrate! You have to fucking concentrate!

Another carbine began to fire from off to the left. Kyle practically screamed in jubilation and relief as rider after rider fell from the saddle in a deadly rhythm. As the last raider slid from his mount the remaining dogs continued to run unimpeded.

Kyle gave a victorious whoop in celebration.

Percy saved the day! He actually saved the fucking day!

It dawned on him that he might have misjudged the man.

I have to admit that it was some of the best damned shooting I've ever seen.

The rangers took the lightly wounded rider as a prisoner and swiftly eliminated the others. It amounted to cold blooded murder in the sense of modern warfare, but Kyle could not afford to guard them all back to the company. Anyone left alive was sure to bring more enemy down upon them. The prisoner was no more than a teenager and scared more than anything else. To Kyle, it seemed that this was his first real fight.

Welcome to manhood you son of a bitch.

Kyle directed for the rangers to start moving the prisoner as he continued to look for Percy. To his surprise Taulk appeared from the left flank holding a carbine at the ready. Kyle stopped, looked questioningly at the native, and pointed at the weapon.

"Where did you get that?"

Taulk had a somber look on his face.

"I am sorry."

Without knowing why, Kyle was alarmed by the statement.

"What do you mean 'sorry'?"

Taulk simply walked toward him with a look of severe anguish on his face. Horrified, Kyle watched the native step slowly down the sand and gravel toward him. The ranger looked at the fallen enemy scattered all the way up to the nearby rise. The native turned back to Kyle with pain in his expression.

"I am sorry."

Kyle felt all the energy in his body drain and he just looked at his friend. Suddenly it dawned on him.

Oh my god - you killed Percy!

A cold chill rushed through Kyle at the supposition and he became light headed.

What am I going to do? What am I going to do?! I can't believe he killed! What the fuck am I going to do?

As he looked behind Taulk, Kyle was astonished to see Percy storm down the slope.

"He can shoot! That man can shoot! Who taught him how to fire carbines!?"

The staff sergeant was drenched in sweat and he had numerous scratches across his face and hands. With an accusing finger jabbed at Taulk, Percy vented his fury with the full force of a megalomaniacal hurricane.

"Who taught you?! *Who!?*"

The dread in Kyle was swept away with a rush of pure relief. He practically laughed out loud on discovering that Percy was still alive. The staff sergeant stormed up to the native and snatched the carbine away, bellowing,

"Who the *fuck* taught you how to shoot these?!!"

Kyle watched Taulk's affect darken, and fearing the man might actually do something drastic murmured a didactic warning. Hearing this, Percy spun with his rage unchecked and practically spit in Kyle's face.

"YOU!?! You taught them?! You disobedient fuck! I'll have your head for this! You'll never see the light of day once they put you in the hole. Hell, the Lieutenant will have you dragged outside and shot if I have anything to say about it!"

Kyle almost laughed at the notion but said nothing as there would be no point. In fact, in the scheme of things he was beyond caring what the man had to say. Percy turned to the other rangers who were scattered around them in a loose circle and held the carbine aloft as he screamed.

"Who else? Who else knows how to use these?!"

The rangers all glanced at Kyle who only nodded his head. They each hesitatingly raised their hand for the staff sergeant to see. Percy turned on Kyle and stuck a finger back into his face.

"You dead! You get me? I'll volunteer to lead the firing squad myself! Hell, I'll volunteer to pull the trigger!"

Ha, you sanctimonious son of a bitch! You'll have to get in line!

Percy finally fell silent as his shrieking trailed off. The rangers glared at him and Kyle, too, felt his anger return. Remembering the moment before the raiders appeared he stared hard at the red faced man in front of him.

"With all due respect, *Staff* Sergeant, you need to keep your voice down. We need to strip this site and carry off our dead before enemy reinforcements arrive."

Percy appeared to regain some of his senses and started to say something else. Judging by the tone of his voice Taulk cut him off by pulling a wicked short blade and holding it suggestively. It was clear that the native had had enough of the soft man from headquarters.

"Staff Sergeant, if you threaten the Corporal again or make another noise louder than a footfall, I'll end you."

Alarmed at the escalation, Kyle was shocked to see Percy take a startled step back and level his carbine at Taulk.

"I'd kill you before you had a chance."

Taulk simply stared the man down.

"You think I'm the only one?"

Percy quickly looked at the other rangers and finally recognized the open hostility they had for him. His carbine barrel slowly swung back and forth as if trying to decide what to do next. The senior man started to panic and croaked,

"You're going on report, mister! This is mutiny!"

Taulk smiled the darkest smile Kyle had ever seen.

"You can't file a report if you don't make it back."

Kyle looked at Taulk in growing alarm.

He means it. This is getting out of control. I have to do something.

Straightening to his fullest height and assuming the best impersonation of Holly that he could muster, Kyle barked at Taulk,

"That's enough of that. Fall out and get the men moving, we're un-assing this area immediately."

Taulk kept his eyes locked on Percy but the smile left his face and the blade was lowered to his side. Kyle became worried that he would not be able to regain control.

Taulk, for the love of Christ stop fucking around and go already!

Kyle leaned toward the ranger.

"I said *move*, Taulk. *Now*."

The native glanced at him before turning to get the squad ready to depart. Percy lowered his weapon as he perceptively deflated with relief. Kyle watched the natives move off like a well oiled machine and turned back to the staff sergeant.

I'm not done with you yet.

"Staff Sergeant, you file that report if you want to; Just make sure you include the parts where you ran in the face of the enemy and Taulk fired your *abandoned* weapon in the defense of the squad. I'll make sure the Lieutenant knows that ranger prevented the escape of the surviving cavalry and that the patrol was compromised due to your deficient skills. I am hereby taking back command of *my* squad, and *you* are more than welcome to join us."

Kyle did not wait for a reply and spun with a hand signal to Lemm. The ranger pulled the bound and gagged prisoner to his feet and led him away. Two other rangers reached down and grabbed the litter on which they had placed Neel's mangled body. With an anger that burned, Kyle shook his head and silently fumed.

If that ranger had been issued a carbine he never would have been close enough for a dog to chew on him!

The others had finished stripping the enemy of intelligence and valuables. As one, the squad spread out in column and moved to the cover of the pines from which they had just arrived. The patrol objectives had been met, but until they made it back to the base, the mission would not be over.

Regardless of the outcome of this mission it wasn't worth the life of one of my men.

Percy simply stood dumbfounded as the rangers continued on their way. Kyle looked at him from the passage point while Taulk counted the others off of the ambush site. The big man signaled the head count and at a nod from Kyle faded into the pines behind the column.

Kyle scanned the surrounding ridges and made a silent prayer that there were no other enemy scouts above them. It would be easy for unfriendly eyes to watch every move they made since the patrol entered the depression. The only hope was to pull back to where the cavalry could not pursue them and make it to the company without being followed.

Percy struggled in a winded huff as he caught up to the patrol. As he slipped past Kyle, his anger and hostility had returned and he hissed in a threatening tone,

"You haven't heard the last of this you little shit..."

With a red face the man trudged past the last ranger who waited to cover the rear. A thought popped into Kyle's head so quickly that he almost laughed at it.

I should do us all a favor and just shoot him now.

The ease with which the notion had arrived alarmed him and kept it from being funny. Kyle had to just wait and see what the staff sergeant would do when the patrol returned to the main post. With a deep sigh he slapped a reassuring hand on the last ranger and headed up the valley after the others.

* * *

CHAPTER IV

Holly leaned forward on the desk as he read through the After Action Report. Kyle noticed that he held a crude cigar in his left hand which he occasionally stuck in the corner of his mouth. The sweet smell of the smoke reminded Kyle of black cherries.

Must be something the locals brought in.

Holly flipped the page over and read the few remaining words Kyle had written before setting the paper down.

"So Evans, you seem to be a magnet for trouble."

Kyle was not quite sure what his platoon leader was getting at and so he remained quiet. Holly looked at him and gave a small laugh.

"Since we've been here you've been in three separate engagements. If I am not mistaken that makes you the most experienced veteran I've got."

Kyle had never thought of it that way.

I guess I am. Dumb luck?

"The good news is that you're still in one piece and you managed to come away from this latest scrap with only one killed."

Kyle swiftly acknowledged the statement and thought about Neel. Ever since that first night, the native and Lemm always wanted to know more about the drop ships. The young ranger had always hoped to see one up close or even ride it one day. After the squad had buried the body, Taulk had presented the family blade of the fallen warrior to Kyle.

At first he refused to take it, but the others insisted. By honoring the weapon, the family was thus honored; Kyle had little choice in the matter. Reluctantly he held the dagger in his hands and clung to it for most of that night. He tried to remember the face of the warrior it had belonged to so as not to forget.

"I lost a good ranger out there, Master Sergeant."

Holly appeared to mull this over and then slowly nodded his head.

"It's not easy losing people in combat."

"No, Master Sergeant."

Holly leaned back, his mouth a grim line across his face.

"In the old days, during the beginning of the Riots, they pulled us kids straight out of the military prep schools and put rifles in our hands."

Kyle looked up from the spot on the desk where he had been staring.

"Three hours later there we were, near the center of the city behind barricades of razor wire. To our front, several thousand pissed off looters came around the corner - and let me tell you - we all wanted to run; Somehow we managed to stay put, afraid to be the first to admit we were cowards."

Holly took a long draw of the short cigar and let the sickly sweet smoke roll out from his mouth.

"There were two hundred of us when it started. Those crazed people ran right up to us and someone in the ranks opened fire. We just started mowing them down as fast as we could. They just got really pissed and pressed forward. Once we ran out of ammunition they took the bodies of the dead and dying and threw them onto the razor wire to weigh it down."

Kyle looked with appraising eyes at the man. Holly just paused and played with his cigar between his fingers.

"At that point there was nowhere to run. We were just a bunch of terrified kids left to the mercy of a crowd gone berserk. By the time they were done beating and clubbing us, you'd have thought we were all dead. The whole barricade was covered with broken bodies and washed in blood. When the reserve battalion arrived, they dug through the pile and pulled out thirty-two of us that were still breathing. In the end, of the original two hundred, only twelve of us made it out in one piece."

Holly pointed to the large scar over his left eye.

"That's where I got this. That kind of experience forces you to grow up real fast, and colors your view of the world for the rest of your life."

Shocked, Kyle could only nod his head in response.

"Your recon patrol killed twenty-two of the enemy, you brought back a prisoner, and some intelligence items of high value. I know that none of this equals the life of a man you served with, but considering how it could have ended it didn't turn out so bad."

Kyle nodded his head again and thought of the snarling dogs whose razor sharp teeth had disfigured Neel. He relived a trace of the raw terror he had felt during the fight which sent a slight shiver down his spine.

Holly blew another thick smoke cloud before stabbing the cigar out in an ash tray.

"How did Taulk get Staff Sergeant Percy's carbine?"

Kyle shot a glance at Holly who continued to rub the crumpled cigar stub without looking up.

"Well, Master Sergeant, I don't really know. Staff Sergeant Percy and I split up at the base of the embankment as I stated. I was shooting targets as they came my way and then pressed forward to rejoin the squad, which had ambushed the enemy from the rear. I heard the other carbine when I tried to stop the cavalry from retreating. It wasn't until later that I learned it was Taulk doing the shooting and not the Staff Sergeant."

Holly looked up from the ash tray.

"You included all that in your written statement. What I'm asking about are the parts you didn't include in the report. In particular, you training rangers to fire carbines and Staff Sergeant Percy running from the enemy."

The senior man stared at the trooper across the desk as a painful silence filled the room. It was all Kyle could do not to lose his composure; he did the only thing he could think of.

He feigned surprise.

"Master Sergeant?"

Holly stared straight into his eyes.

"Natives don't pick up a carbine for the first time and drill bad guys out of the saddle at sixty yards without someone showing them how to do it. Staff Sergeant Percy changed his story so many times, the only thing that is clear is his weapon somehow magically appeared in the hands of your ranger."

Kyle stared at the man, unwilling to dig a deeper hole but also unable to just come clean. Holly appeared slightly irritated.

"Son, I want to explain something to you."

Oh shit, here we go.

Kyle could feel the tension. A good number of ass chewings began this way.

"I don't want someone out there leading soldiers who can't do the job. I want to know, right *now*, if Staff Sergeant Percy ran from the enemy. 'Yes' or 'no'."

Kyle started to answer but lapsed into silence. He hated the staff sergeant from the core of his being. The trouble was that two years in the infantry taught him that dirty laundry should be kept within the unit. As far as he was concerned the matter was concluded unless Percy was again assigned to lead his squad.

"No, Master Sergeant."

Holly seemed perplexed at the response.

"If he didn't run then how did Taulk end up with the carbine?"

Kyle felt his teeth grind. The situation had turned serious and Holly was not going to let it go.

"Master Sergeant, Staff Sergeant Percy and I collided during the initial enemy attack and took a tumble down an embankment. That is probably when he was separated from his weapon. Taulk was out to our left when the fighting started and probably came over to lend assistance when he saw us go down. I suppose that is when he recovered the weapon."

Holly continued to look at Kyle but his gaze was less penetrating. He carefully formed the question and then asked it.

"In your opinion, had your ranger not used that weapon to stop those riders, would your patrol have been in serious danger of being wiped out?"

Without hesitation Kyle answered.

"Yes, Master Sergeant."

Kyle was hesitant to speak his mind but decided that it was now or never.

"Master Sergeant, if my men had been issued carbines like us troopers, we could have easily cut down that cavalry detachment and I wouldn't have lost a man."

Holly gave a slow nod of the head.

"Fine. Just so you know your man was recommended for disciplinary action thanks to your friend Percy. The staff sergeant claims that after confronting the native about firing the weapon the ranger threatened to kill him. What's more, he said you condoned the behavior and did nothing to stop it."

Kyle was stunned by the revelation.

That son of a bitch!

Holly could see the shock.

"Oh yeah. One thing Percy didn't realize is how well I know you and your men, not to mention the question of how Taulk got his hands on the carbine in the first place. Percy's story became full of holes and unraveled shortly thereafter."

Kyle looked at his platoon sergeant with relief.

Thank god he's on our side!

"One last thing; looks like the leader of that cavalry you ambushed had orders on him written in Universal. Seems this almighty 'One' is determined to track down new arrivals at any cost in order to bring us under his influence. The orders contained maps and troop movements for a wing of the Horde and it looks like they're heading our way on the scale of an entire corps of cavalry. Just to give you an idea of what we're up against, the locals claim the parchment is made from human skin. I don't have to tell you about the ink."

Kyle had not seen the orders as they had been snatched up by Percy while the rangers buried Neel. Kyle decided to let the staff sergeant carry the intelligence items hoping it would shut him up for the time being and hopefully for the return trip home as well. It apparently had not.

So I guess we're dealing with a real head job here.

Holly stared at the trooper as the details sank in.

"Okay, fine. Report back to your squad bay and you and your men are to remain confined to quarters until further notice."

That was it. Kyle was surprised the debrief ended so abruptly. He stood, saluted, and exited the office on weak legs.

How is it that I'm still in one piece?

As Kyle approached his squad bay he passed by two troopers from 1st Platoon. He noticed that they quietly veered out of the way, aware that it was out of place for neither to greet him.

They know I'm caught up in something hot again and they don't want to be near the lightning rod during the storm. Percy strikes again.

In the squad bay, his rangers were inspecting their booty, having already cleaned their equipment and filled their canteens. Taulk stood as he entered and Kyle waved the others to continue what they were doing. The rangers were eager to show their take to friends and families. Kyle himself had not grabbed a thing, as his hands were already full at the time. He glanced down looking at the hilt of the family blade, and thought of Neel.

I think I'm already carrying enough of a load as it is.

"How goes it?"

Kyle took a deep breath before he let it out through clenched teeth.

"I don't know. I think that Holly is going to do everything he can for us but we have to see what happens."

Taulk tilted his head right. Kyle looked him squarely in the eyes.

"Listen, I want all of you to answer any question they ask you to the best of your ability. I mean about anything including the carbine instruction and exactly what was said out on that patrol. If these people think we're hiding stuff from them they are going to skin us alive. I think that we just have to put our cards on the table and see what happens."

Taulk gave a gruff acknowledgement and Kyle could tell the others listened in. He found a place to sit and pulled out Neel's blade. As the squad prattled on in their native tongue and sharpened their weapons, Kyle thought about the man who had forged the knife. He wondered about the family of the ranger that would never see their loved one again.

We all should have been armed with carbines.

He did not look up as he spoke quietly to Taulk.

"Back when we first made contact with your people, a warrior was shot and killed after he attacked me. Do you know anything about it?"

Taulk thought for a moment.

"There were a number of hunting parties in the foothills out to search for the dragons. After several nights, word spread of foreign men in a valley of the mountain. This was of interest to us as there had been no unknown people here before."

"Word spread of a warrior being killed by a sling stone of tremendous power. The chieftains grew angry at the fear in their men and assembled the clans to destroy the foreigners and take the weapons for themselves. The one killed was not of great importance. He was just another man passing on in the spirit of a warrior."

Kyle looked at Taulk.

"After we shot the man we had to cache the body in order to come back for it later. When we returned it was gone."

Taulk nodded his head.

"As it was with Neel. We took the body to a safe location and buried it with dignity and prevented others from finding it. After you left, some of the warriors returned and did the same. In all likelihood they were family of the slain man."

Kyle nodded his head and thought back to the fateful moment.

"He died because I accidentally tripped onto him and he thought it was an attack, I think. He jumped me and was kicking my ass when they had to shoot him."

Taulk nodded again.

"It is good to know that a warrior can get the jump on you and fail to kill you."

Kyle was not sure that the one sided fight counted as a fair contest. He had felt the genuine camaraderie with the warriors in his squad and hoped the death of the man would not lead to trouble within the native contingent.

Later that afternoon Kyle tried to explain to the rangers basic infantry principles of the defense. Master Sergeant Holly's arrival interrupted the lesson. Kyle started to rise but was waved back down by the platoon leader.

"At ease, at ease, people….relax."

Kyle and the rest settled back down and all looked at Holly.

"The Lieutenant has come to a decision that all rangers are to receive complete training, equipment, and arms."

Kyle felt a tremendous weight leave his body as he looked skyward.

Thank you! It's about damn time higher made some sense after all!

"On one condition: All natives who want to remain rangers must enlist in the Army for a term of service of at least four years. By this I mean the regular Army, not this motley organization we currently have assembled here. If we ever get off this rock they will come with us. That being said, no native outside the ranks is to be taught nor instructed in any of our tactics and equipment. I catch a trooper doing that, I *will* shoot the bastard myself."

Kyle believed it.

I don't think I'm going to test that threat. But how can they just spot recruit foreigners into the military?

Holly read his expression.

"The Lieutenant has the authority to act on behalf of the Department of the Army in an emergency. Since we have had no contact with any home force since our initial landing, months ago, it has been deemed appropriate to establish an outpost here on this planet until pick-up can be arranged. Until then we will continue to improve our position and influence, as well as hold on to what we've already got."

Holly glanced at the various faces that stared back at him. The senior sergeant looked straight at Kyle.

"Now, since you took the liberty of starting the training, you have been tasked with the responsibility of instructing the rangers in the use of our small arms. That means extra work and long hours. You are personally responsible for making every last member of this company sharpshooters or the Lieutenant is going to handle you by your short hairs."

Kyle acquiesced.

So that's how the Lieutenant would have his revenge — force me to do extra duty. Fine. I'd rather be out there teaching these guys how to fight than shoveling out latrines.

"What's going to happen with Staff Sergeant Percy?"

Holly looked at Kyle and then smiled slightly.

"*Sergeant* Percy shouldn't be giving you guys any trouble. No one tells me a pack of lies and struts away without walking crooked. If he so much as looks at any of you sideways I want to know about it. Perhaps a little more time in the HQ cooker will show him the error of his ways."

Kyle nodded at this as Holly looked at everyone collectively.

"Right now there is a large force of Horde coming toward our mountain chain from the east. The Lieutenant realizes that we can move to good defensive positions and chew them up as they try to enter the foothills, but we're going to need every available man we can get our hands on. With the gross disadvantage the enemy has in numbers, and in light of your recent clash, we'll need a combat multiplier to tip the scales in our favor. Every man with a firearm is what the Lieutenant has decided. Oh, and Evans…? I would stay away from headquarters for the next few days if I were you."

With that Holly departed as unceremoniously as he had entered.

Kyle looked at Taulk who broke into a wider grin.

"Soon I will be a trooper too!"

Kyle smiled back as he slowly shook his head.

"Don't get too excited. I hear it's not all it's cracked up to be."

* * *

The next morning all the rangers reported to first formation and learned about the Oath of Enlistment. It was explained that any ranger who enlisted in the army would answer to the officers and cadre of the unit and not to the local chieftain. Any ranger who had not wished to enlist could still serve in the local militia as a scout or forager. It was also emphasized that should the Fleet arrive to take the company off the planet, all rangers were subject to possible extraction as well.

To the surprise of the troopers every ranger volunteered. Taulk later explained that the Chieftain instructed the natives to serve faithfully with the foreigners in order to become better warriors. In their new capacity the men would learn the ways of modern combat and thus be better at defending their homes and families. Kyle hoped when the Fleet did show up the natives would not be forced to leave their tribes, else there might be a mutiny.

An official Basic Training program for the newly enlisted men began the same day which started with ever popular head shaving. Several days of initial instruction passed without incident. Late one evening, as the hairless rangers rested in their squad bay, a loud noise shook them from their bunks. Kyle recognized the scream of a drop ship landing, and calmed the anxiety of his men as best he could.

"It's alright! Who wants to see a dragon in flight?"

Wide eyed, all of the rangers simply stared at him until Lemm slowly raised his hand.

"Follow me!"

Kyle led the man out to the low berm wall bordering their platoon area and noticed the others following at a slight distance. The high whine of the engines was deafening and the landing lights blinded them. Due to the darkness it was difficult to make out much detail of the craft. Kyle pointed out crew unloading material from the belly of the ship, returning several times for more. Taulk appeared at his elbow and spoke loudly in order to be heard.

"Is that the dragon?"

Kyle smiled and tilted his head in reply. Lemm watched the lights blaze as the troopers moved to and from the beast. The roar of the engines unnerved the other rangers, and the down draft blew stinging gusts of dust into their eyes.

The lights dimmed then disappeared, leaving only the sound of the engines, which increased in intensity. Kyle called out a warning and the natives shielded their faces from the harsh blast of air that followed. With a rush that shook the earth the drop ship leapt into the night sky. Silhouetted against the stars it made a fearsome impression. The rangers took shelter behind the berm with their shielded eyes locked on the monster in flight as it clawed away from them.

The roar and dust cloud quickly settled and from somewhere down the valley a groan echoed back to them. Kyle wondered quietly if it was a technique the pilots had somehow perfected as it sounded all too real.

For a long time afterward the rangers simply stared at the sky where the dragon had disappeared. Their minds tried to process the sight they had just witnessed. Not able to think any further, they rose to their feet without further conversation and walked the distance back to the squad bay in silence. As they climbed into their bunks Kyle doubted they would get much sleep that night.

Kyle walked back outside and squinted up into the sky carefully searching the new constellations for the invisible line he had been tracing each evening. Finding a familiar pattern of stars Kyle noted the galactic progression and made a rough estimate. Waiting intently for several minutes the specified light wobbled suddenly and disappeared. Grinning to himself Kyle felt some connection to their new planet and the heavens over it.

I know where you are!

* * *

The next morning after first formation the rangers were marched to the company Armory. Kyle halted his men and they awaited their turn to enter. At that moment a squad of warriors marched past singing an old native chant. When Kyle looked them over he understood why they were so happy. He gently tapped Taulk on the shoulder and pointed out that which the rangers carried.

Each of the warriors had a brand new rifle cupped with his left hand and braced against the same shoulder. Even though Kyle was not familiar with the longer rifles he knew exactly what Lieutenant Taylor had done.

The drop ships each had an internal module to support the different battalion level shop tasks. If the unit was left to operate independently of other resources the modules would allow the troopers basic critical services. From what Kyle knew the company had a Medical, Machining, and a Decontamination module available. It appeared the Lieutenant fired up the machining unit and cranked out a bunch of small arms for the rangers.

The squad was placed at rest with Taulk left in charge. Kyle was required to report to the Company Armorer, Sergeant Sanchetti. Once the other squad leaders had assembled, Sanchetti began his class.

"Alright, listen up. I am Sergeant Sanchetti and this is Specialist 5 Lewis. We will be your instructors for this block of instruction."

Lewis was standing off to the side in a position of at ease. His eyes briefly swept across the troopers assembled there.

Kyle did not know him well but had seen him around the compound on several occasions.

"Today you will receive instruction on employing and maintaining the X12 Single Shot Air Rifle."

Single shot? What the hell is this?

Lewis held up the new weapon for the troopers to see. It was longer than the carbine by half a foot and a little more bulky. The stock was more pronounced and across it was a leather pocket holding eight individual projectiles. Sanchetti continued to speak.

"This weapon fires the standard issue combat projectile utilized by your carbines and machineguns."

Lewis pulled a projectile out of the pocket holder and held it up for all of the troopers to see.

"This was done to simplify supply and make your squad firepower cross loadable."

That's good. This way we can break down a projectile belt or brick and have enough ammunition for everyone.

Lewis took the projectile and placed it back in the leather stock pocket.

"Your carbines and machineguns are equipped with a Rapid Compression Unit. The RCU is what sucks in the atmosphere and builds sufficient pressure to force the projectile down the barrel and then chamber the next round."

It was an ingenious design of the weapon. Instead of hauling around explosive powder to create the pressure an

RCU would do it instead. That being said, Kyle had no idea how the unit actually worked.

I'm just like my rangers. It's just another magical wonder of the modern age.

Sanchetti continued,

"The X12 does not have an RCU. The reason for this is that they are extremely difficult to manufacture unless in ideal conditions and at this point we do not have the sufficient raw material to make many of them. Instead, the firer will charge the weapon with a manual step up. He will do this by pressing the release on the side of the rifle."

Sanchetti paused briefly as Lewis tilted the weapon so that the troopers could see. He pressed a lever with his thumb on the neck of the stock where it met the receiver of the rifle.

"He will then take the weapon by the forward barrel grip and the base of the stock and charge the weapon by 'breaking' it toward him."

Lewis took the barrel in his left hand where it had external grips designed into the surface. With his right hand he held onto the butt of the stock which was shaped in such a way so as to give the firer a superior hold. Pulling the ends toward him Lewis 'cracked' the rifle in half on a hinge joint.

Kyle was not the most technically minded individual but the design made sense. This way a ranger could benefit from the strength of both arms to charge the main cylinder. In the event one of his arms was injured the soldier could still cock the weapon by placing the butt into his stomach and pulling with the remaining good arm.

"The X12 is designed to benefit from a hydraulic step up mechanism that achieves a ratio of twenty to one. This means that for the thirty pounds of pressure required to charge the weapon, the projectile will leave the barrel with six hundred pounds of force per square inch behind it."

This surprised Kyle. It was the equivalent of having the tip of the projectile balanced on your chest and the force of six hundred pounds dropped onto the base. Without a doubt it would easily penetrate the human body.

To reinforce this point Lewis inserted a projectile from the stock bandolier into the exposed chamber of the rifle. He then snapped the weapon closed by reversing the breaking action. He held the weapon in a firing position pointed safely off the stage. It was then that Kyle noticed a set of native armor wrapped around a large sand bag to the right.

"Demonstrator, fire when ready."

Lewis pulled the trigger.

BLAM!

Kyle observed minimal recoil and a firing report much deeper than the high crack of the carbines. The armor, which consisted of a shield and chest plate, jumped slightly with the impact of the projectile. Lewis held the weapon at port arms before placing it onto the makeshift table in front of him.

"Notice the lower report of firing. This is due to the lower PSI of the X12 compared to our carbines and machineguns. Even though the X12 packs much less penetration power you will note the effectiveness of the shot."

Lewis stepped over to the armor plate and slid it up and off the huge sand bag, propping both the shield and chest plate on the table for the troopers to inspect. Kyle could clearly see a pattern of holes in both items from this, along with previous, firing demonstrations. Specialist Lewis was only two holes away from completing a nice smiley face.

I definitely wouldn't want to be on the business end of one of those!

Sanchetti continued.

"The sand bags are filled with a mixture of bone and moist clay that resembles the density of a human body. You will notice that the shot failed to exit the sand bag."

Lewis held up the back plate of the armor which had no mark on it.

"This is the desired effect, as it means the projectile carries sufficient energy to penetrate the protection of the target and imbed itself inside the vital organs. It also guarantees a complete transfer of the projectile energy to the target and thus a greater chance of achieving a knockdown."

To Kyle the information was important to digest. His carbine could fire a projectile through two targets before burying itself in the third. Understanding the different capabilities and characteristics of the weapons would be crucial in determining where and how to deploy them.

"The projectile does not have the power to penetrate our standard combat plate armor. This ensures that any friendly fire or captured weapon fired at you will be defeated. This does not guarantee that the path of deflection will be safe since you are not wearing a full protective envelope."

Kyle exchanged a look with Corporal Wilcox sitting next to him. The mortar man raised his eye brows and shook his head soberly.

"The maximum effective range for a point target is two hundred meters. Again, the intent of the X12 is to give the native soldier a weapon that can out-perform the standard issue missile weapons they may come up against."

The next half hour passed with Lewis demonstrating sustained rates of fire and basic weapon maintenance. After Sanchetti answered general questions from the gathered troopers, each was given the opportunity to fire the weapon several times. When his turn came, Kyle found the cocking and loading a bit awkward, but gained a healthy respect for the accuracy and stopping power of the new rifle.

It's not a carbine but it sure beats the hell out of using a hand axe!

Upon returning to his squad Kyle took charge and marched the group over to the armory window. Each man beamed proudly as he was issued a new weapon, and Kyle could not help but smile himself.

It's just like Yule back home, with presents for everyone.

The rangers then marched to the firing range where Kyle demonstrated and instructed them on the proper firing technique. The next few days were spent plinking targets allowing the rangers to master the flight of the projectiles. Being that there were no bad habits to break, most of the men easily qualified with their weapon on the first try. Taulk and several others even made Expert with a perfect score at two hundred meters.

The rangers were then issued a basic load of sixty projectiles, bandoleer, cleaning kit, helmet shell, and combat web vest. Kyle showed the natives all the tricks and techniques that he knew for keeping the equipment in good working order. The natives eagerly absorbed every last detail and continued to hone their skills.

A few weeks passed and Kyle was reviewing the upcoming training schedule with Taulk when word arrived. One of the drop ships had been conducting high altitude reconnaissance sweeps to the east. The Horde had continued a steady advance across the steppe toward the mountains. Within several days the van of raiders would reach a small village nestled in a mountain pass. The only way to cross a large body of men over the steep foothills and into the valley beyond was through that village which dominated the terrain.

Historically the Horde would pass by the region every couple of years. Traditionally, the villagers would pay some form of tribute to escape the destruction wrought on the surrounding farms and people.

The rangers were traditional hunters and nomadic, so they would simply move inside the protective mountains whenever the Horde reared its ugly head. Even so, there were a few large raids that would strike deep into the valley. Most of the rangers had family that had suffered in one fashion or another from the living plague.

After more than a century of predictable calamity the Lieutenant finally decided to alter the natural order of things.

In order to stop the Horde from spreading into the valley and threatening the main post, the company had to occupy and hold the village in the pass. If the Lieutenant wanted enough time to prepare a defense he needed to conduct an emergency air assault within the next twenty-four hours.

Due to the nature of their traditional role the rangers were light on their feet and ready to move at a moment's notice. Once Holly received the order he directed Kyle's squad to join the rest of the platoon at the pick up zone. There the squad was given a chalk number which was the order in which they would load the drop ship. In the distance, the roar of engines rumbled up the valley and the rangers gathered behind Kyle in growing anxiety. This would be the first time they got to see the dragons up close and personal.

As the drop ship hopped up from behind a low rise to the south, Kyle turned to the men and signaled for them to stand. He made one last quick inspection to ensure all was in order and ready. The drop ship checked its descent and landed heavily on the flattened grass about fifty meters away. The shockwave of debris and dirt belted the rangers where they stood crouched against the gust.

The waist doors of the ship slid open as a crew chief stepped down the ramp to the ground and gestured to the Load Master. The Load Master turned from his position, pointed to Kyle, and signaled him to advance. Kyle ran up to the Load Master, confirmed his chalk number plus headcount, and then turned to motion Taulk and the rest of the squad forward.

Eyes wide and hands in a death grip on their rifles, the rangers obediently proceeded as one. It was obvious that the repeated rehearsal of mock loading and unloading in the squad bay allowed the petrified natives to keep their legs moving forward. It was the most frightening experience of their lives to date. Kyle led them at a quick pace toward the waiting doors and a free ride to the east.

As they neared the drop ship Kyle glanced at the fuselage and noticed a large playing card painted below the canopy of the craft. Above it, lettered in a swirling script, was painted the word *Joker*. Further forward a large serpent eye and half of a demonic grin completed the picture. From a distance it did indeed give the impression of a large beast looking for some mischief to inflict.

The Lieutenant would not be amused, but under their senior officer the aviators and crews vigorously made known their Fleet command structure was independent of the infantry. Although the two groups were quick to assert their professional barrier, this did little to effect the mutual support required for their joint survival.

The crew chief waved Kyle and the chalk into the troop compartment past a waist gunner sitting near the opening. The man wore a darkened helmet visor, sported a weak mustache and enjoyed a wad of something that was stuffed into his cheek. Inside the drop ship Kyle quickly led the rangers down the first available row of troop seats and settled them in. Even though he had rehearsed the strap down procedure with Taulk previously, it took a quick demonstration for the native to finally understand how to maneuver the various straps. Working in concert the two made quick work of their task and headed for their seats at the head of the row.

Kyle locked Taulk in and ensured all rifles were snug in the holders. Satisfied that nothing would shake loose during the flight, he sat down in the squad leader chair on the end and strapped himself in. Securing his helmet and donning the headset stored on the headrest, Kyle could hear the cross chatter of the crew as they finalized loading in order to begin their preflight check list.

"Chief, how many more we got coming on this run?"

Kyle glanced outside to his left at the crew chief who looked at a small data pad clipped to his chest.

"Looks like two more chalks, Boss. We're not hauling any equipment this run either so we're good to go after this."

"Roger Chief, tell them ground pounders to hurry it up or we'll make 'em walk the whole way."

"Roger."

The crew chief motioned vigorously to the last ranger chalks approaching the ship. Kyle glanced up toward the crew compartment doors that led to the cockpit.

Kind of a cocky little group now aren't we?

Previously, Kyle had seen a few of the flight crews around the company compound when they were between missions. There was more of a laid back attitude between the officers and enlisted men. Then again, there were only eight members assigned to each drop ship. As the only Fleet representation, they became a very tight knit community.

The last chalk which was lead by Rogers stumbled past. After a minute he reappeared and took his seat in line with Kyle. Holly came through the waist door and greeted the crew chief with a fist pound. Kyle grinned at this and could see that the man had a good rapport with the flyers. The platoon leader made several quick spot inspections before locking himself into a chair at the front of the compartment. Holly donned and then adjusted his head set whilst addressing the pilot.

"JOKER, this is ROMEO, we're in and ready to roll."

The crew chief also keyed his microphone.

"Roger Boss, we're good to go."

"Roger. Stand by."

With that the engines of the drop ship whined to full power. The frame of the craft shook with the intended effect of unnerving the rangers inside. Kyle felt his irritation rise.

Son of a bitch! It's hard enough to get these guys into the damn ship in the first place and you just have to torment them!

The crew chief smiled from his seat, and again, keyed his microphone addressing the nervous squad leaders to his front.

"Hang onto your seats boys, we're going for a ride!"

The man hit a button on the console overhead and loud heavy rock music blared out from the speakers in the bay. With a thundering roar the engines drove the drop ship skyward with a crushing force. The rangers inside clung desperately to anything they could get their hands on despite being strapped in. The bored expression on Holly's face did not change a bit as he sat through yet another joy ride provided by the rocket jockeys up front.

During the entire ascent the only thing Kyle could hear over the music and engines were the terrified screams of the rangers trapped helplessly inside.

* * *

CHAPTER VII

The village started out as an outpost on the edge of two frontiers. To the west was an awesome valley carved by a river flowing due east which marked the southern border of the settlement. The water merged with another river from the north, which made the eastern border, and then both flowed to the south. From the north, steep rock faces that were nearly impossible for any man to climb, ran south and parallel to the western bank of the water. To the east, as far as the eye could see, was a steppe of shoulder high bluegrass.

The drop ship *Joker* landed several miles north of the town, along a path that led to their destination. The idea was to preserve the shock effect of the ships for as long as possible. Regardless, Kyle was sure someone would see the screaming beasts land and the legend of dragons would persist.

The overall plan had each of the three drop ships making an insertion to the north, south, and west of the village which would allow for first hand reconnaissance of the terrain. Leaders took meticulous notes as their patrols plodded through the rough, broken ground of the foothills toward their objective. The southernmost group crossed a series of rough wooden bridges that spanned the valley river just before it merged with the other bordering the steppe.

Lieutenant Taylor had officially reorganized the company into two separate task forces of three platoons each. The first task force was composed of one platoon of troopers and two platoons of rangers who were left behind to guard the main post and interior of the valley. The second was composed of two platoons of troopers and one of rangers that would be deployed to defend the mountain pass from the advance of the Horde.

The organization of the Pass Task Force made sense to Kyle as it allowed two modern platoons to fight forward with the ranger platoon held in reserve. This enabled the natives to plug gaps in the line as well as free them up for special missions as needed. Holly selected the squad position along a ridge that led up to where the mortars would be deployed. The location of the holes would cover the rear approaches to the village and provide over-watch of the two platoons which were in line on the eastern slope of the village.

The natives, with the help of the villagers, dug their fighting positions. Holly was ordered to provide a security screen out in the tall grass to the east. The rangers, arranged in a wide arc, allowed for the detection of infiltration parties that might be probing ahead of the main enemy advance.

Kyle noted more often that his equipment was starting to show signs of wear and tear from extended field use. In the event that communications failed altogether, the rangers were instructed to fire on any enemy sighted, and withdraw while remaining in contact if practical. Any uninvolved rangers would immediately file down their side of the screen and exfiltrate to the defensive perimeter. There the natives would wait for those in contact to make their way out while providing cover fire as needed. The ranger platoon would then pass through the other two platoons in order to occupy battle positions to the rear of the main defensive line.

Holly kept in contact with the squad leaders via the helmet radios for most of the deployment into the steppe. He kept the platoon frequency in their right ear and task force frequency in their left. Occasionally Kyle heard Percy on the task force band as a radio operator stuck in headquarters. Kyle smiled at the thought of the sergeant invisibly chained to a transmitter where he could do the least harm.

By rights the son of a bitch should be dead.

On the morning of the second day Kyle walked his picket line when the task force frequency crackled to life in his left ear.

"TITAN 6, this is JOKER, OVER."

Kyle halted mid stride to listen as one of the drop ships called from high overhead. Even though he knew he would not be able to see it, Kyle looked skyward anyway.

"JOKER, this is TITAN 6 ZULU, go ahead, OVER."

The voice of Sergeant Percy was easy to distinguish.

"6 ZULU, Contact report follows, prepare to copy, OVER."

After brief moment of silence, Percy spoke again.

"Go ahead JOKER, OVER."

"Approximately one thousand November Mike Echo; Grid Foxtrot Bravo fo-wer fo-wer tew, six fife tew; Moving Sierra Whiskey on a heading of tew tew fife degrees Mike. They look like mounted cavalry and appear to be moving at a fast march pace, OVER."

A thousand enemy cavalry were spotted somewhere to the northeast and bearing down on the ranger screen. Based on the grid reference, Kyle looked at his map and figured the Horde to be no more than fifteen kilometers away. Percy read back the contact report to the pilot who confirmed it.

"6 ZULU, tell your actual that at their current rate of speed they will over take your ROMEO elements before they can make it back to the nest. JOKER requesting fire mission for harassment and interdiction, OVER."

The pilot wanted to use the mortars to break up and slow the enemy cavalry in order to give the rangers time to make it back to the main defense line in the village. Kyle stared off to the northeast as he listened, even though the source of the contact was well beyond anything he might have been able to observe. In front of him was nothing but flat kilometers of man high grass for as far as the eye could see. Somewhere out there a large force of mounted raiders wandered toward him.

Kyle had his rangers posted on small knolls they had made from stacks of sod cut out of the steppe. The slight elevation helped a little with visibility, but still they were not very high.

If the bad guys knew where the ranger positions were, they could easily dismount and crawl undetected between the observation posts. Holly figured the Horde mentality was based on safety in numbers and a reliance on brute strength rather than stealth. This meant the enemy would most likely remain mounted and visible to a drop ship perched overhead. When Kyle inquired as to why the rangers were still being deployed in a screen Holly reminded him that 'likely' did not mean 'definitely'.

The task force net crackled again.

'JOKER, this is STEEL 6 ZULU, send your fire mission, OVER."

It was on!

STEEL was the call sign for the mortars on the ridge behind the town. Kyle wished that he could see what was about to unfold. Apparently the Lieutenant had approved the fire mission request. Some dog mounted hostiles were about to get pounded into chopped meat. The platoon frequency crackled in his right ear.

"ALL ROMEO elements, this is ROMEO 6. Move to Phase Line Charlie, I say again move to Phase Line Charlie, acknowledge, OVER."

Holly had ordered the ranger patrols to pull back to the defensive line just east of the village as there was no need for the early warning patrols anymore. When it was his turn, Kyle acknowledged the order and set off at a quick pace toward the next observation mound.

On the task force frequency the fire mission was underway. The pilot of *Joker* finished his initial request and adjusted the first spotting round onto the target.

"Add 1200, Right 800, OVER."

Kyle cringed as the initial spotting round was well off the mark. At the extreme distance of over fifteen kilometers, it was understandable since the only fire support available to the defense was the organic company mortars. Regardless, it was an impressive range to be able to reach when attempting to kill the enemy. Wilcox, in the mortar Fire Direction Center, echoed back the adjustment request to the drop ship pilot.

Kyle stopped moving long enough to listen for the mortars firing the adjusted round. Even though he strained, the only sound he heard was the soft wind moving the thick blades of grass dancing around him. He continued to hustle toward Taulk and the others.

"Drop 400, and Fire For Effect, OVER!"

"Drop 400, and Fire For Effect, OUT."

The second spotting round landed close enough to the enemy. The pilot was not going to try and bracket the target with a third adjusted round, and took a shortcut for the quick kill. Kyle came upon his first observation mound and ordered one of the rangers to spread the word down the line to Taulk. Everyone was to file back immediately and head for Phase Line Charlie as soon as possible.

As Kyle paused to catch his breath, he briefly thought about the dogs who panted their way under masters toward the death that was soon to find them. The riders probably heard the initial spotting rounds and saw the marking smoke, but they could not possibly know what was headed their way until it was too late.

Boy, are they in for a rude awakening!

"JOKER, 6 ZULU, Wun Tew rounds, OVER."

"Roger, Wun Tew rounds, OUT."

The wind died down at that moment as if it knew a show was about to start. Kyle raised a hand to silence Teek who nervously studied the tall grass to their front. Kyle turned to the distant west to listen for the distinctive sound of twelve mortar shells leaving their tubes. A compression round assist helped to make the journey to the extreme range of the weapon's capability. Kyle could barely hear the faint but distinct sound of the firing.

poomb *poomb* *p-p-poomb* *p-poomb* *p-p-p-poomb* *poomb*

Wilcox came back on the company frequency.

"JOKER, Rounds Complete, OVER."

"Roger, Rounds Complete, OUT."

The mission had been fired and the mortar shells arced their way toward the target. Kyle leaned back and stared straight into the sky as he searched for the black dots which sailed over his position. Teek stood nearby and looked questioningly toward the strange sound coming from the village, and then copied Kyle as he scanned the air above them.

"Corporal, what are you looking for?"

Kyle realized his search was futile at such a range and turned to the young native. He could see the nervousness on the face of the warrior and forgot that his rangers had no helmet radios, and were thus unaware of what was happening.

It's hard being the lowest guy on the totem pole and having no clue what was going on.

"Sorry Teek, I forget to keep you guys updated about things that I hear on the radio. We have large rifles called mortars which were firing at the lead elements of the Horde. When the big projectiles from the mortars hit the ground they explode into hundreds of little projectiles and kill everything around them."

Teek appeared surprised to learn of such a thing. Kyle reflected on the incomplete training his rangers had received, and wished he had had more time to prepare them. Unfortunately, The One had decided not to accommodate them and started his attack several weeks too early. Teek looked curious.

"Where are these mortars?"

Kyle jerked his thumb over his shoulder, back toward the pass.

"Remember where we dug our position in the village? Higher up on that same ridge. The mortars are firing their projectiles at a high angle all the way over there."

Kyle pointed in a rough northeast direction.

"Somewhere out there is a large group of Horde riders headed this way. One of the dragons is telling the mortars where to shoot in order to break up the enemy before they can reach us."

Teek appeared to consider the distance to the village. Then he turned and looked out past where Kyle had pointed.

"Mortars can sling projectiles that far?"

Kyle nodded his head and grinned at Teek who wore a mask of disbelief.

"There are bigger guns that can sling much larger projectiles even further than that. Unfortunately we didn't have any of those with us when we arrived on your planet."

Teek was stunned.

"Even further than the mortars?!"

Kyle tilted his head in the native fashion.

It's got to be a lot for his mind to process. Then again they are like children learning of our world for the first time. Once you explain things to them they seem to accept it and move on.

Teek looked perplexed as he scanned the sky around them.

"Where is the dragon now?"

Kyle laughed slightly as he pointed straight up.

"Somewhere up there beyond our visible range. They float in the air and tell us the movement of the enemy so that we can make better plans to defeat them."

Kyle watched as the young ranger scanned the heavens above for the drop ship. Teek started to ask another question but Kyle silenced him with a gesture as the task force frequency crackled once more.

"6 ZULU, RIGHT 200, Fire for Effect, OVER!"

Wilcox echoed back the adjustment. From the sound of it Kyle figured the pilot waited for the cavalry survivors to regroup and shifted the adjustment right on top of them. Kyle used pieces of sod on the ground to help explain to Teek what was happening.

"Okay, the dragon just asked for the mortars to fire more projectiles at the enemy, but in a different spot."

Kyle then pointed back toward the village and waited expectantly.

poomb *p-p-poomb* *p-poomb* *p-p-p-poomb* *poomb* *poomb*

Kyle imagined the devastation to the battle hardened raiders on the receiving end. He contemplated the angry buzz of the metal shards, blown at high speed, piercing men and dog as easily as a knife through butter. The result of such an attack was a completely shredded and scattered enemy. There was no way to fully describe the effect to Teek, so Kyle did not try. He made a mental note to get his rangers up to speed with the Call for Fire procedures when they resumed their training.

I'll have to show them a little example later on. That is, if we make it out of here in one piece!

As his rangers trickled in, Kyle continued to monitor the mortar fight against the cavalry. *Joker* continued to work the pattern of fire that he had used earlier. It was a truly brutal tactic to use against an enemy who grouped together for mental safety, inadvertently providing a bulls-eye to strike.

Kyle signaled the squad to move out. The rangers each glanced at his face trying to read how the fighting went. Teek explained what he had learned to the others, but he was clearly frustrated by his own inability when it came to answering their questions. Kyle counted each of his rangers as they quickly filed by. Bringing up the rear he ensured that no one was left behind.

I'm down to nine now. I wonder how many I'll have left tomorrow?

As the patrol made its way toward the low, dark foothills the firing of the mortar tubes grew louder. Kyle kept a sharp eye out for the shapes of raiders in the tall grass. It was possible for some advance scouts to have made it that far on foot, and he vowed never to be surprised again. Briefly he touched the torn copy of *The Killer Angels* in his pocket where he had kept it ever since that day.

By the time the squad moved a kilometer toward the village perimeter, *Joker* called an end to the fire mission which silenced the mortars. The pilot estimated a body count of around six hundred enemy cavalry. The rest scattered into small groups that fled to the north and east. For all intents and purposes, the unit ceased to exist as an effective fighting force.

The squad spent the next half hour making their way back through the grass. They paused long enough for Kyle to set up trip flare wires behind them at specified intervals. When the patrol neared the village the vegetation suddenly stopped. It had been cut flat for half a kilometer in every direction, radiating out from the river junction. The villagers who stayed behind removed any concealment the enemy might utilize in order to sneak up on the defensive perimeter. Eager to keep their skin on their bodies and their homes intact, the men worked tirelessly with their scythes and carried the stacks of cut grass behind the village to be used as forage for livestock.

Kyle called in a situation report to Holly and informed the platoon leader that the squad had reached the site identified as part of Phase Line Charlie. This was a trace of the edge of the cut portion of the steppe. Holly acknowledged and instructed Kyle to continue into the defense network to occupy the assigned squad positions. Up the slope leading to the ridge, he made out the mortar positions against the mountains in the distance.

As the squad made its way closer to the village they passed through a series of angled split log spikes sticking up from the ground. The tips were sharpened and meant to impale any cavalry that attempted to charge straight across the low flowing river in order to hit the east side of the defenses. Behind the spikes was the bank of the river from which any sort of large cover had been removed. Although the flowing water was shallow enough to wade across, the slippery stones, which lined the bed, made for treacherous footing. This would provide another obstacle to infiltration and direct assault.

The river bank closest to the village was covered by a series of machinegun positions. These were located where they would provide maximum grazing effect of the projectiles by firing them a meter off the ground for the distance of the mowed grass. The penetration power of these heavier throwers would be more effective at cutting down the large dogs that were sure to fill the plain.

Above these machineguns were the individual fighting positions for the rest of the respective platoons. They were placed in a lazy zigzag pattern around the edge of the village to form the main line of defense. The arrangement of the holes allowed for mutual fire support to each of the neighboring positions, while providing cover and concealment from enemy observation and arrows. Most importantly, the platoons would be able to fire on anything that approached the machine gunners, keeping those critical weapons safe from being overrun.

All of the fighting positions had overhead cover made from dirt piled on thick tree trunks, which gave good frontal overhang. This meant that an arrow had to be fired at a flat trajectory in order to enter the firing aperture. Enemy bolts loosed from across the river would arc too high in their flight and strike the overhang or the ground in front of the troopers. If the enemy closed in for a melee, it would be forced to lean into the muzzles of carbine fire in order to reach the occupants.

The village itself had also been prepared for the coming battle. All roads and trails that led to the buildings were blocked by sharpened felled trees known as abatis. These protections were under observation and fire of the troopers in the defensive positions. The women, children, and elderly were moved under armed escort away from the village itself and taken to a temporary camp further to the west. A unit of scouts was assigned the responsibility of protecting the civilians until it was safe to return home. The able-bodied men formed militia units. They were armed with crude pikes and would concentrate on manning the buildings of the village which were converted to impromptu forts.

The rangers passed through the anti-cavalry fence and by way of a narrow log bridge covered with a layer of gravel, crossed the shallow river. The Lieutenant had ordered all other crossings removed, and had left this one intact to help draw the enemy advance into the main kill sack of the defensive plan. After all friendly units were west of the river, the gravel would be removed and grease applied to the timbers. This would make for a visually tempting passage point that would be less than cooperative once gained.

As the squad crossed over the flowing water, Kyle could see the troopers of the regular platoons working in, and around, their fighting positions on the eastern slope, just outside of the village. Someone stood on top of a machinegun bunker and waved. Kyle returned the greeting unsure who it was at that distance.

They walked up the main trail to the first outlying buildings of the village and wove their way through a series of additional abatis obstacles meant for just that purpose. Once the rest of the defenders were finished outside of the perimeter they, too, would pass through this same point. The main road that led up to the barricade would then be blocked with additional abatis.

The barricade itself was a high wall of earth and logs manned by a unit of militia. The local men kept watch at the entrance of the village searching for any spies that might try to mingle with the population. These guards stared at Kyle and the rangers as they passed through the gate giving only a slight dip of the head in acknowledgement. Occupation of the village by all the rangers and troopers of the task force must have unnerved the townsfolk, but Kyle also understood their fear of the alternative. A visit by the Horde would be devastating. He glanced down at his own combat load as he trudged up the trail and his eyes fell to Neel's dagger which was sheathed under his left arm.

Kyle instructed Taulk to lead the squad to its position while he stopped in to report to the task force command post. Headquarters was situated in the corner of a large walled-off courtyard which had originally been intended as a safe haven for the villagers. For the upcoming fight the solid stone structure would serve to protect the nerve center of the defense, and serve as an Alamo if the need arose.

A new corporal took the report and made an entry in the task force log. Kyle wondered silently who would read the log book years from now, if it survived that long at all. As he glanced up, he caught Percy who briefly looked at him from where he sat in front of a transmitter. In apparent disregard the sergeant simply went back to his work. Kyle just smiled and headed out the way in which he had come.

It's probably best that he isn't going to be near me for the fight, else I know where my first two shots would have gone.

When he arrived in the platoon assembly area Kyle checked on the rangers. They conducted personal maintenance and inspected their ammo, medical, and food supplies for the upcoming battle. He was not sure how long the engagement would last, but once they got into their holes he was going to do his damnedest to make sure they had no reason to get out.

With one last look back over his defenses, he watched the last of the ranger patrols filter in across the area of cut grass and head for the foot bridge. Kyle knew it was only a matter of time before the next people coming from that direction would do their very best to kill him.

* * *

CHAPTER VIII

"IRONMAN, this is EAGLE, OVER."

Kyle woke with a start. Next to him Lemm glanced over before he returned to his task of watching the terrain from the fighting position they shared. Kyle cleared his head with a small shake and squinted through the firing port of the bunker to see a star laden sky.

"EAGLE, this is IRONMAN, go ahead, OVER."

"What is your current location, OVER?"

"At my Charlie Papa, OVER."

"Roger. Will be at your position in fife mikes, OUT."

It seemed Lieutenant Taylor wanted to see Holly for a face to face discussion. Kyle pulled himself up next to Lemm and once again peered out of the firing port. He could see the shape of the Lieutenant, with another trooper in tow, emerge in the starlight as they walked toward the ranger platoon headquarters. Kyle sat on a ledge in the bunker and rubbed his blurry eyes.

"Anything interesting happen while I was out?"

"No, Corporal."

Kyle soured as he wondered where all the bad guys were. Despite the fact the *Joker* had switched out of the rotation with the *Ace*, a low, dense fog had obscured the view of the steppe for the first half of the evening. There had been plenty of opportunity for the spread out enemy to converge on the village. He glanced at his helmet radio and noted the time to be twenty-one forty-two hours.

If only they'd hurry up and get it over with!

Kyle turned over and dug into a haversack for a piece of jerky. The warriors brought the technique for preserving meat with them, and after a short while the troopers became believers in the tough, flavor-laden ration. At times Kyle could feel his mouth begin to water just thinking about the dark strips of protein.

As he stared out over the steppe, a flare suddenly shot skyward far out in the low ground fog. The bright green light glowed with intensity and hung for a few seconds before it burned itself out.

As his heart quickened, Kyle tossed the haversack into the corner of the bunker and leaned on the sill of the firing window. The green trip flares were placed at one thousand meters, with yellow at seven fifty, and red at five hundred. Something in the grass and had set one off.

It could be an animal, or a civilian wandering through the area unaware. Maybe it's just a false alarm.

In rapid succession, green flares leaped into the night sky across the whole arc of the extended perimeter.

Wild animals my ass…!

Kyle turned to Lemm.

"Keep your eyes out there and stay put. Do not shoot until ordered."

The ranger tilted his head absently as he placed his rifle on the sill and stood up on the firing step. Kyle rushed out of the bunker to the next fighting position in his squad defense. He dropped to a knee next to the firing slit, and called inside,

"You guys awake in there?"

"Yes!"

The voice was excited but under control.

"Okay, don't do anything until you hear from me. The only time I want you to start shooting is if enemy start flooding over that barricade to our front. I don't want you guys hitting any of our friends down there."

"Understood, Corporal!"

Kyle looked down to the main barricade built across the east end of the village square. From there the militia watched the colored flares fade from the sky. These ordinary men had the responsibility of controlling the center of the village and defending it against all attack. Most did not have their crude pole arms with them and only a few were on top of the makeshift wall.

Kyle worked his way down past the other positions in his squad and repeated his instructions before returning to his own hole. As he started to head into the entrance, a sudden swish of yellow flares lit up the steppe in almost perfect unison. Kyle backed out and stared in sudden alarm.

There's no friggin way that's wildlife!

Holly crackled in his helmet.

"Net Call, Net Call, Net Call! All ROMEOs sound off!"

In sequence, each of the squad leaders acknowledged the alert. Kyle tried to figure out how much time had passed between the two sets of flares. He came to a determination and realized that whatever tripped the warning was moving fast!

"All ROMEO elements, stand by –"

Within seconds red flares streaked into the night sky and a terrible roar of thousands of voices rolled out of the now blood colored steppe. A wave of mounted raiders emerged at full gallop onto the edge of the cut grass field and headed straight for the village. The light of the last flares colored the black clad enemy in an evil red glow and gave the impression all hell had broken loose.

And then suddenly it had.

Kyle dove into his firing position as the machineguns at the base of the slope opened fire in unison. He pulled himself up to the firing slit as he watched the first wave of riders go down just inside the kill zone. There was a series of mortar thumps from off the ridge and he tilted his head to try and see the shots going out. Several tiny suns blazed to life from under parachute canopies and lit up the surrounding terrain with their man made daylight.

The sheer volume of fire from the company machineguns was fearsome. For a brief moment Kyle felt pity for the hapless dogs caught in certain death, as the roar of the charge quickly dissolved into startled yelps and cries. A second wave hurdled over the first destroyed line and quickly closed the distance to the river.

After a brief loss of rhythm, the machineguns picked up their steady cadence and chopped into this new line as well. Kyle and Lemm watched in fascinated horror as an endless ripple of enemy tumbled to the ground under the relentless pounding of projectiles. Cries vanished in the throats of the dying, while the steady machineguns hammered out a beat of death.

An irrational third wave advanced closer. The cavalry spikes waited patiently for the massed charge to impale itself. Kyle quickly figured that at the present rate of carnage it would take another ten waves of cavalry for that to happen.

That's just insane! No one could take that kind of punishment and hope to be effective once they reach our positions!

Down below, the machineguns continued their steady, deadly thump and the Horde continued to die. A fourth, fifth, and sixth wave pressed to within three hundred meters of the perimeter, and the troopers in over-watch began to add the fire of their carbines to the slaughter. The mortars on the ridge lobbed high explosive rounds at the enemy five hundred meters away in an effort to break up the weight of the attack.

To Kyle, it seemed an unstoppable living ocean of black and red rising up to kill them. The swell of screaming and dying continued as men spurred their dogs closer to the river. Simultaneously machineguns and carbines knocked and punched them to the ground in rapid succession. Kyle felt the fear build within him.

They're just going to keep coming. There has to be thousands of them!

Holly crackled into his helmet.

"Evans and Rogers! Grab up your people and report to my hole on the double!"

So much for staying in the damned bunker!

Kyle acknowledged and beckoned Lemm to follow him. As they passed the other fighting positions, he told the young ranger to assemble the squad and meet him at the platoon command post. Kyle hustled up to the doorway and noticed Holly listening intently to a radio. The sound of heavy carbine fire served as background to a frantic transmission.

"…all over the ridge to our north. I have a thin security screen out there now but things are getting worse by the second! Those people are going to push us off this hill and roll us up from the flank, OVER!"

Holly nodded his head absently as he keyed the microphone on his desk.

"We're on the way. Tell your boys to hang tight and we'll be right there, OVER."

Without waiting for a reply Holly turned to Kyle and Rogers who just arrived.

"Mortars say they have a mess of infiltration from the north along the ridge. Apparently some scout element worked its way up and around the line on our left flank. The tubes have a security screen out, but they are fighting for their lives and are in serious danger of being overrun. You two get up there with your people, report to Grissom or Wilcox, and kick those sons a bitches off of my ridge!"

Kyle and Rogers acknowledged, and backed out of the bunker to collect their respective squads. Both groups then ran full tilt up the steep rise to where the mortars continued to fire their deadly mission into the steppe. To the north, the distinct sound of carbine fire could be heard above the general din of battle far below.

Rogers automatically maneuvered his line left and Kyle took his rangers to the right. The squads came on line and rushed straight toward the mortar pits and crew. Far below on the steppe, another enemy charge ran headlong into the meat grinder. Kyle noted that the enemy was almost to the cavalry spikes. The Horde appeared to be using the sheer volume of their casualties to help screen and protect their advance forward.

How can they afford to fight like this? How many lives can they just lay down to get to us?

As the rangers approached the tubes, Kyle could see several troopers forty meters beyond who fired from a hastily dug trench. The handful of men attempted to pin down the entire ridge which now crawled with enemy. The crews on the tubes maintained their steadfast discipline and ignored the threat that closed in on them from the endangered flank.

Kyle gestured to Taulk and the squad moved to take up positions amongst the beleaguered security element. As each ranger dropped into place he shot anything that moved to his front with a steady hammer of the rifle. Kyle added the rapid fire power of his carbine, and the enemy push was driven back leaving a number of dark figures littering the ground. One crazed raider, several meters from the trench, charged forward while brandishing a wicked looking blade and bellowed in blind rage. Kyle silenced him with a neatly placed shot to the forehead and yelled to no one in particular,

"Scout element my ass! The whole damned hill is crawling with these fuckers!"

Wilcox appeared and chimed in from a spot next to him.

"You can say that again! We were just getting ready to dance with these mothers when you guys showed up!"

They both poured rapid fire into the enemy as quickly as the raiders showed themselves. A brief lull presented itself and Kyle called Holly on the platoon frequency.

"ROMEO 6 this is 2 – it's a concentrated push up here with the mortars but we are holding them at this time, OVER."

Wilcox picked up several grenades which he armed, and threw, in rapid succession toward the nearby rocks. Kyle did not bother to duck down as the grenades sailed out and landed in a small depression a safe distance away. The blasts ripped any enemy hidden there, and forced the survivors back, or out, into the open. Wilcox quickly cut them down.

"Yeah! Yeah! Little bastards like to group up there and make a rush for our holes! I flush them out every once in a while to keep them from becoming a real threat!"

The man seemed to have aged since the day at the rifle demonstration. With the effects of the constant fighting and tough living, Kyle would have easily mistaken the teenager for someone ten years older.

A sudden swish in the air near his face caused Kyle to duck out of reflex. A second affront struck the lip of the trench, behind which he was positioned, followed by another that deflected off his helmet. Startled, Kyle lost his balance and landed in a heap. He quickly regained his footing and fired a quick succession of shots in the direction of the attack.

"What the fuck was that?!"

Wilcox did not even look up as he continued to fire into the darkness beyond.

"Arrows! The fuckers have a ton of them too! They'll probe for a bit and when we knock them back enough they fire a hail of arrows at our position to –"

A wet thunk was followed by a sickly gurgle as Wilcox went down. He fell to the floor and writhed momentarily in the low light of the hole. Kyle moved to lend aid, but a sudden cry heralded a new attack. With the appearance of a new line of enemy, he was forced to turn and open fire.

After the fifth shot the carbine was emptied, and the feed chamber door locked open. Kyle fumbled for another brick of projectiles from his ammo pouch, but dared not take his eyes off of the enemy line as it advanced.

Don't panic, focus, don't panic, focus!

By the time he slapped the brick into the feed chamber Kyle knew he would not be able to stop the advance. The steady pounding of rifles from both flanks reminded him that he was not fighting alone. Most of the enemy were cut down and Kyle fired on the survivors who tried to make it back to safety.

That was too close! We need more carbines!

Kyle quickly slung his weapon across his back and struggled to position Wilcox where it would be easier to evaluate the wound. The head of the man fell back limp and exposed vacant eyes which stared at nothing. Kyle looked down and saw a black shaft protruding from his throat. Kyle could have made a call to Doc Roberts but it appeared that, even now, it was too late. From behind him another battle cry raised from the rocky darkness.

Son of a bitch! Don't you fucking people ever quit!?

Kyle reached down and tossed the remaining grenades that Wilcox had with him. The steady explosions and hard clap of concussion only hinted at the damage inflicted on the enemy. Kyle only stopped tossing grenades when the box was completely emptied. He took up the dead man's carbine and bandoleer before hugging the edge of the trench.

As the dust and smoke settled, Kyle could hear the occasional rifle and rapid crack of carbine fire from his flanks. Around him the ground was pierced with scattered arrow shafts. As far as his low light visor would allow him to see, a carpet of dead led back to the enemy-held portion of the ridge. With at least a hundred casualties the enemy pressure appeared to be spent.

Kyle looked back to the fight down on the steppe and was shocked to see the entire mowed area filled with black clad enemy. The warriors had advanced across the center of the small river in a steady solid wall, as bodies floated with the persistent current. Although the machineguns still tore at the masses of enemy, the assault continued to press forward and gained the near the river bank.

The mortars behind him paused briefly to adjust their rounds closer to the fighting positions. Kyle watched as a shell was dropped down a tube. The mortar belched and far down below, a geyser of dirt, water, and enemy was flung skyward. Kyle almost fired from his position but decided against it.

I'll deal with them if they get closer. Besides, there might be plenty more of their buddies up here!

With a cautious glance toward the shadow of the enemy ridge Kyle made his way over to Rogers. Along the way he passed several rangers and Taulk, to whom he handed the extra carbine and ammo bandolier. The native looked at it questioningly.

"Wilcox is dead. Put these to good use."

Taulk tilted his head and slung his own rifle across his back. Further out, Kyle came upon Rogers who had a black arrow shaft protruding from under his left arm. The wounded man seethed as he looked up at Kyle.

"I was fucking pointing, and the assholes shot me in the friggin' arm pit!"

Kyle looked at the wound while Rogers winced and clenched his teeth.

"You going to be okay? Do we have to get you back to the aid station?"

"It just fucking hurts like a bitch is all. I'm fine, I'm fine!"

One of the rangers at the site snapped the remaining length off the shaft and leaned the wounded trooper forward. A nasty barbed arrow head along with the proximal end of the shaft stuck out from between the shoulder and back plates of the body armor. Bright red blood covered its length and ran down Rogers' web vest. He flinched with pain and anticipation of what was to come next.

"Son of a bitch! Son of a *bitch*!"

I hope to hell these aren't poisoned.

From behind Rogers, the ranger masterfully plucked the shaft free in one deft motion. Rogers barely shifted in response. Kyle reassured the wounded man as they applied pressure bandages to the injury.

"It looks alright. You're going to be okay. Try to move the arm as little as possible and keep an eye on it or you might bleed out."

Still experiencing the pain, Rogers nodded with his jaw clamped shut while fumbling for his carbine. Kyle looked back down the ridge toward the enemy that now pressed against the outside of the village defenses. He was alarmed that he could not hear any of the machineguns firing.

"Listen - I'm going to leave my wounded with you and take some of your men back down to reinforce the village. Those bastards are dismounting and pushing up to the barricade and the militia are going to break for sure. I have to get down there to hold the line or we're going to get rolled!"

Rogers nodded his head again and was helped to the edge of the shallow trench. Kyle moved back along the line and pulled any able bodied ranger he passed along the way. As soon as the perimeter security for the mortars had been reestablished, Kyle led his force down the slope at a run. Black arrows dotted the landscape and continued to clatter by at irregular intervals.

As they neared the platoon command post, Kyle signaled for the squad to take shelter near an adjacent building. Holly emerged from the bunker, took Kyle by the shoulder, and pointed at the village square below.

"The barricade, get your men to the barricade! The enemy is pressed up beyond the machineguns and the militia is getting their clocks cleaned!"

Holly produced a heavy satchel full of fragmentation grenades which he handed over. Kyle took the strap of the bag and passed it over his shoulder. The corporal turned to the rangers assembled there.

"Bayonets! Fix Bayonets! We need to drive them off the barricade!"

The natives grabbed their blades as they followed him down the steep cobblestone road. Kyle ran as fast as he possibly could toward the barricade, countering the heavy weight from the load in the satchel. As he neared the wall, the militia threw down their pikes and fled from the enemy who peeked out over the top. Scattered around the base were several dead and wounded villagers.

You have to give them credit for holding out this long!

Kyle led the charge of rangers straight up to the barricade. He halted just out of reach of the enemy blades and tossed several grenades over the top in a rapid succession. On the other side of the wall the bulk of enemy troops took the full force of the explosions.

The rangers arrived a moment later and fired point blank into the faces of the raiders. With their initial volley expended, the squad vaulted over the top of the wall. The grenades had torn large gaps in the press of enemy which supported the main assault. The natives hurled themselves onto the retreating raiders with bayonets and rifle butts.

Kyle tossed the satchel aside, brought the carbine up to his shoulder and fired on a mass of enemy climbing the house to the left of the barricade. In rapid succession, the black clad raiders fell back howling onto the masses below. Kyle continued to fire while perched on top of the barricade, as the rangers drove the enemy down the road toward the abatis. A raider, who earlier had feigned being wounded, jumped up and lunged at Kyle only to receive a carbine burst at point blank range to the chest.

The road that led to the barricade was a quagmire of fallen and retreating enemy. The rangers formed a line at the base of the wall and laid down a steady volley of fire that physically drove the raiders away. Taulk stood in the center of the group pouring rapid fire with Wilcox's carbine, dropping several attackers with each shot. Kyle noted grimly from the top of the wall the effectiveness of the weapon.

If not for that one carbine those guys would probably be overwhelmed by now. I have to get them better firepower!

Unable to face the sheer destructive power of their advanced foes, the surviving raiders fell back in shock and horror. Seeking relative safety the enemy gathered at the road barriers. Enfilade machinegun fire began again from the left flank and caught them by surprise. Kyle immediately ordered the rangers back to the protected side of the barricade and provided covering fire. The natives collected themselves and their wounded. As the last man reentered the defenses, Taulk crouched nearby to load another brick into his new prize.

"I like rifles but these carbines are king!"

Kyle gave a quick grin and peeked back over the wall to check the flanks where the barricade met the houses on either side. The right was clear, but the left still had a large number of raiders pressed against it. Kyle threw his last two grenades into the mass of bodies and called to Taulk.

"You keep the squad here and firing down the road. Hold this position at any cost while I go check on this flank."

The grenades detonated as Taulk directed the rangers at the top of the barricade. Kyle climbed down from the wall and glanced along the road that led behind the two platoon positions to the north. The din of battle could be heard from every quarter as he made his way into the adjoining house which was occupied by members of the 2nd Platoon. There he discovered Sergeant Dunn and another trooper who fired at the mass of enemy gathered at the reinforced windows.

Dunn stepped aside in order to reload his weapon. When a man appeared at the firing slit, Kyle impulsively shot the attacker in the face. He yelled to Dunn as he fired intermittently through the window.

"We managed to push back the breach on the barricade!"

Dunn finished loading his weapon with an alarmed look on his face.

"Breach? Good thing you were on it because we didn't even know it was happening! They could have just swung around behind us and got us from the rear. I told Holly that the militia would break first chance they got!"

A spearhead on a long shaft slashed the air between their faces. Dunn instinctively grabbed hold of it while Kyle fired his last three rounds into the wielder. Dunn pulled the long weapon inside the room and tossed it onto the floor next to several others.

"We're holding them here but the 1st Platoon is getting the shit kicked out of them! The machineguns stopped firing a while ago and the enemy line appears to be anchored past the forward positions!"

Kyle listened to the only machineguns he could hear, which were those located in front of 2nd Platoon. If the 1st Platoon positions further down caved, the whole task force was in danger of being rolled up and wiped out. Thinking quickly, Kyle yelled to be heard.

"Listen! I'll get with Holly and see about forming a mobile reserve in case we need to counter attack a break through! Right now I've got my rangers on the barricade so you don't have to worry about your flank anymore. Let me know if you need any assistance."

Dunn nodded his head as he dropped a grenade out the window into the yard below. The fire along the entire 2nd Platoon line increased heavily as a large wave of the Horde pressed toward the flank of the machinegun bunkers. The black cloaked men were slapped and knocked to the ground in a hail of deadly fire which hit them from every angle. Kyle ran back to Taulk and the other rangers who still fired steadily from the top of the barricade.

God bless them, they're really holding their own up there.

Kyle rested with his back pressed to the barricade and called for Holly on the platoon frequency.

"ROMEO 6, this is ROMEO 2, OVER."

He got no response. Kyle cast a brief look up toward the platoon headquarters and saw activity there. The mortars continued to fire from the ridge beyond. Kyle reached up on tiptoe and slapped Taulk firmly on his calf in order to get his attention. The ranger stopped firing long enough to bend down to listen.

"You hold here! I'm going back up the hill to talk to Holly and see about forming a reserve in case there is another break through to our left! You're in charge until I get back!"

Taulk nodded his head and returned to firing as another hail of black arrows rained down upon them. Kyle dodged past militia men, who carried away their own wounded, and ran up the hill toward the platoon command bunker. His earphones crackled with cryptic messages on both frequencies and it was hard to understand what was going on. Lieutenant Taylor was heard at brief intervals inquiring about a possible penetration of the 1st Platoon line.

Kyle made half the climb before hearing a deep rumble originating from the far left flank. He looked over and could see a large stream of flame that lashed out of the perimeter to engulf the attackers. Several more spouts of hell ignited the raiders who collapsed or ran trailing fire. The large black cloud of smoke that rolled skyward was under lit by successive bursts from the weapon.

Flamethrower! That ought to put out some heat!

In one receding motion, the enemy moved down the slope away from the captured positions for which they had paid so dearly. With the initiative regained, troopers emerged to take back the holes they had been forced to abandon. The massed carbines poured a withering fire into the retreating enemy, who broke even faster and ran for the river bank. Most did not make it.

From the darkness of the steppe, deep horns heralded the retreat. The shattered forces turned away and left an ocean of their fallen behind them. The river piled bodies into a small dam and water overflowed the banks. The mass exodus across the kill zone was peppered with the occasional mortar blast or spray of machinegun fire. The troopers continued to shoot along the entire front until no visible target could be seen.

His task momentarily forgotten, Kyle stood on the road that led up the hill and watched the secondary fires burn on the 1st Platoon slope. High over head another illumination round glared into existence and swung slowly across the black sky trailing a cloud of putrid, orange smoke behind it.

From all directions the ground that led to the village was a carpet of bodies. Scattered throughout were heaps of enemy formed as they fell climbing over the wounded and dead in front of them. Only the occasional shot could be heard over the general moans from the fallen; it was the sound of a broken enemy.

Someone called down the road from above him, and Kyle turned to see a trooper with his helmet askew. The man was caked with soot and blood. Only the whites of his eyes betrayed mortality.

"You know where Corporal Evans is? Master Sergeant Holly is trying to reach him on the platoon frequency!"

Kyle gave the trooper a thumbs up and keyed his microphone.

"ROMEO 6 this is 2, OVER."

After a brief pause Holly replied.

"2 this is 6, all ROMEO troopers are to assemble at my position as soon as possible. Put your number two in command of your squad and order him to hold the line until further notice. The rest of us are going on a raid. 6, OUT!"

Kyle quickly trotted down the hill to the squad and found Taulk with the others as they laid out several bodies at the foot of the barricade. Most were militia but three were rangers. His heart dropped when he noticed that Teek was one of them.

The face of the young man was smudged with dirt and blood. A dark trail in the corner of his mouth ran toward his ear. Kyle kneeled next to the body and could see several large stab wounds to the chest and abdomen. Taulk came and stood beside him.

"He just kept advancing until they overwhelmed him. I think he had a blood lust or refused to halt the advance. There was nothing we could do as they overpowered him."

Kyle simply stared at the face which was now eternally free of pain. He then searched the body with his eyes in a slight panic.

"What happened to his…?"

Taulk held out the sheathed blade to Kyle.

"I was going to honor it unless you would like to do so."

Kyle stared at the weapon then gently pushed it back.

"No. You were his team leader. You honor him."

Taulk nodded his head and fastened the item to his waist belt. Kyle placed a hand on the shoulder of the dead man as a sign of respect and stood up. He looked up and could see the surviving rangers keeping watch outside the barricade. He regarded Lemm who only stared back at him.

At least I didn't lose all of them.

Kyle turned and walked slowly away as he motioned Taulk to his side.

"Secure the squad and hold here until further orders arrive. The troopers are tasked with a raid of some sort. It seems we're going to go pay the Horde a visit."

Taulk tilted his head in acknowledgment, stopped, and then saluted. Kyle was surprised by the formality but halted and returned the gesture. Taulk grinned warmly and then left, leaving Kyle alone with his thoughts.

At the rate I'm losing rangers there won't be much left for him to lead.

A drop ship roared down onto the low hill behind 1st Platoon. It kicked up dust and fanned the scattered flames that still burned there. The area looked as though something monstrous had chewed up the surface and spit it back out. The fight at the barricade was a close thing, but Kyle could tell from the burnt homes that 1st Platoon learned a hard lesson and paid for it in spades.

As he jogged up the hill to join Holly, Kyle wondered how many of the troopers were saved by their armor and carbines. He brooded over the thought of how many of his rangers would still be alive had they been provided with the same equipment.

* * *

CHAPTER IX

Kyle was actually relieved that his rangers would not be on the raid. He had lost too many of them already, and their lack of armor and weaponry troubled him deeply.

How can you lead a bunch of men and not share in the same risks that they are willing to take?

Back in the assembly area, it felt odd to be with a team composed entirely of troopers again. The last six months had been a growing experience. How many times had he and his rangers prowled the mountains armed literally with only cloak and dagger? Now he sat in his body armor with a full combat load, preparing to board a thirty ton drop ship.

Most of the ranger cadre had been tapped for the mission, with the exception of Rogers. Doc Roberts was concerned that one of the trooper's arteries, nicked by the removed arrow, might be subject to hemorrhage with any additional insult placed upon it. He did not want to risk it bursting. The wounded Rogers instead found himself as the acting platoon leader for the rangers left to guard the village and he welcomed the challenge.

Kyle fell in with the others assigned to his chalk and together they conducted pre-combat inspections on each other. He thought of Teek running into the sharpened blades of the raider line and shuddered involuntarily.

That's not going to happen to me.

Once their equipment was checked the troopers lined up to board their ride. It was only a few minutes before Kyle picked out the second craft as it materialized in the early morning light.

The ship came in over the steppe which was now littered with the bodies of the dead and dying. Dogs howled in pain and whimpered until they were put out of their misery. The death and destruction was horrible for most any man to witness, but there was something about the cries of the dogs that really got to him – it did not matter that they were the size of bulls.

The *Joker* came in and slowly spun sideways and offered an open waist door to the waiting troopers. The pilot balanced the craft so that only one side touched the steep slope while expertly floating the other.

The crew chief waved them on, and Kyle followed the others into the troop bay. They quickly and quietly strapped themselves in, stalwartly quelling their trepidations over the task at hand. Kyle placed his carbine in the holder and squeezed into the seat. He suddenly felt caught in two time frames: the present and the past, when they had made their initial landing. It was an unnerving deja vu.

No matter when you go, there you are.

The entire assault element loaded and moved out in less than two minutes. The acting squad leaders checked their troopers before strapping themselves in. Once completed, Holly got the okay; using his microphone he communicated with the pilot. A moment later the drop ship lurched upward and the engines whined to full power as it clawed for altitude.

Holly's voice came in over their helmet headphones.

"All right! Listen up!"

All heads turned toward the front where the senior man sat.

"We've had a little taste of what these supposed bad boys can do. They showed up uninvited to our barbeque and we kicked their asses."

A couple troopers hooted and hollered. Kyle recognized that too many had just lost buddies and most only hoped to see the sun rise again. Death had a way of quelling bravado.

"Here's the deal:"

"Situation: There is a large enemy force approximately four hundred and thirty klicks east of us. They appear to be a mix of fifty thousand infantry and twenty thousand cavalry."

Kyle thought back to the violent brush with the cavalry patrol in the mountains. He briefly wondered what would have happened if Percy had lead the rangers back at the Pass.

Had he been in charge I know the mortars would have been lost along with the barricade. The whole flank of the task force would have crumbled and the rest of the positions would have been rolled up.

"Reconnaissance has identified what it believes is the headquarters element of the Horde army."

"Mission:"

Kyle and the troopers automatically echoed with a loud, unified voice.

"MISSION!"

It was a technique used to force troopers to pay attention to the most essential part of the orders process.

"The platoon shall conduct an air assault raid, no later than ten hundred hours Zulu, at grid Foxtrot Tango tree, tree, six, fower, fife, sero, in order to find the son of a bitch responsible for all of this and capture him."

Holly reiterated the Mission statement a second time.

Kyle was surprised to be part of the main effort to capture the commander of the enemy force. Never one to think of himself as a Special Forces type, it humbled him to feel the weight of responsibility now placed upon them. He wondered what the man would be like or if it might possibly be The One himself.

Whoever he is, the guy hasn't won any popularity contests.

Holly then explained the concept of the operation as he saw it. The troopers were broken down into the different chalks to be loaded into the separate drop ships. The air assault would utilize speed in the descent on the enemy headquarters encampment. The drop ships would break at maximum flare, their engines stirring the opposition into a panic and clearing the landing zone for the assault.

Once on the ground, four designated machinegun teams would occupy the corners of the landing zone and drive back any organized enemy response that might be moving to counter the insertion. An assault element would then enter the headquarters compound and grab the target and any intelligence items of value. All other enemy personnel were to be eliminated and any remaining materials destroyed in place, where possible. The raid would conclude in less than five minutes.

Joker and *Ace* flew to the designated link up location just under an hour away. Kyle thought about the crews, of which the average trooper saw very little. Most of the time the drop ships either conducted orbital recon or hid deep within the mountain cavern to await their next mission.

How much harder would our lives be if we didn't have these guys and the ships to support us?

Holly gave the alert as they approached the remaining drop ship for a mid air rendezvous near the release point. The crew of the *King* had made the initial reconnaissance flight which located the extent of the Horde and identified the critical command and control encampment. Kyle and his chalk were assigned to the *King* as part of the assault element. They grabbed whatever equipment they deemed necessary for the mission ahead and got to their feet.

The two drop ships linked up in flight and a secure connection was established. Once the chalk was seated aboard the *King*, Holly spoke a few words into his microphone before sliding the headset down to his neck.

"Alright assault element – listen up!"

Holly placed a large digital pad on the seat in front of him where everyone could see it. The display showed an aerial view of a series of tents surrounded by a high sod wall. It resembled a sports stadium and looked as if it could house around a hundred enemy.

"This is the target area."

Holly passed his hand over the mass of tents in the rectangle.

"Every night the raiders stop to make camp and the leadership has them throw up a sod fort cut from the steppe. The bosses spend the night inside, in relative safety, until the morning at which time the whole operation is broken down and the Horde moves on. This is what we're going to do."

Holly picked up the tablet, sat in the seat, and placed the display back onto his lap.

"Since we have no idea where the leadership is during the day, we have to wait for them to stop for the night. They'll congregate and make it easier for us to grab the target. Since they are on full alert at sun up and sun down we're going to hit them in the middle of the night."

Holly stabbed his finger at a tent roughly centered in the compound.

"This is where the head man should be. Most of his cronies will be spread out in a circle around his tent with the boot lickers gathered near the walls on the outside. Each sub boss will probably have some sort of personal security detail of thugs, so expect fanatical responses once we set foot in the compound. Don't play games with them. Just shoot the bastards until they stay down."

Holly then pointed to a specific point on the wall halfway along the shorter edge of the rectangle.

"The drop ship will offload us out of the waist door and we will occupy the tops of the walls. Any enemy personnel are to be cleared to make way for the machinegun teams so they can get into position. These teams will face outward and blast everything they can see. Our job is to focus on the interior of the fort and grab the head guy. Remember, if it isn't the man we're looking for, or an intelligence asset, then you shoot or burn it until it is destroyed. Clear?"

Kyle and the other troopers all nodded an affirmative and gave a small grunt of compliance. He briefly thought back to the previous fighting and how the raiders rode straight into the machineguns. He wondered if the big wigs were as rabid as their foot troops.

"The drop ships will then circle in a low wagon wheel around the fort perimeter using the down blast of their thrusters to scare off the cavalry. Waist gunners will provide additional fires to help eliminate counter attacks that might endanger the mission."

Holly glanced up from the data display and briefly scanned the eyes of the troopers gathered before him.

"Get your heads straight boys. Some of you just survived the first real fight of your lives. Now I need you to get ready for your second."

Holly continued to speak and added new emphasis.

"We are the assault element. We will disembark and immediately move to take the central tents. Wilson, Hicks, and Brando will go with Sergeant Higgins. Miller and Regis will handle prisoners. Quinn and Lansing are aid men; Torres and Logan will place demo on order. Richards, Evans, and Chen are with me as the grab team and need to draw assault pistols. We do nothing but look for the head honcho. Everyone needs to remember that carbine fire will penetrate the target and pass on through. Make sure your field of fire is clear before pulling the trigger."

Kyle was surprised to be selected for the grab team. It was the group charged with greatest responsibility. The Master Sergeant had probably selected him because of all the hand to hand training they had done together.

That's what I get for becoming so familiar to the senior sergeant.

Holly looked at him.

"Questions?"

Kyle shook his head no but several others raised a hand. Kyle half listened as he thought back to the endless hours of instruction from Holly. The beatings he had taken, the endless pointers, and all of the coaching were now ingrained in his head. Kyle recalled the nameless man who had almost strangled him to death. Surely that man was more of a warrior than Kyle ever was. The assault element was about to take on thousands more just like him.

The questions ran out and Holly assembled his team to rehearse entry and movement techniques. He made several spot corrections on the proper handling of the pistols each had received. Kyle was responsible for refreshing the team on several hand-to-hand quick-kill techniques. He unsheathed Neel's dagger and demonstrated some knife strike tactics as well. Something about holding the blade gave him a little more confidence.

Once Holly was convinced that the grab team would not shoot each other he left to inspect the others. Kyle and the troopers tightened their armor and adjusted their equipment for the hundredth time before finally dropping into their chairs and strapping in. Richards talked about nothing in particular as he practiced fast-drawing his pistol.

Holly then personally scrutinized the troopers and their restraint system. He ensured they could free themselves with a single pull of the release strap. Satisfied, he made his way back to his seat at the head of the bay and put on his head set. He called out to them in a bellow loud enough for all to hear.

"Lock and load!"

Each of the troopers slapped an ammo brick into his carbine and chambered the first projectile. Since this would be a hot landing zone, Kyle and the others would not lock down their weapons, as with a reentry. Instead they would keep the muzzle to the floor where an accidental discharge would not take out any critical systems on the drop ship. Kyle contemplated a projectile ricochet in the bay and cringed at the thought. Such were the risks run going into combat.

Holly held a thumb up to the members of the assault element. Kyle and the other troopers returned the sign and the senior man reached up to his helmet and slipped it on. He secured the chin strap and gave the crew chief the go sign.

Kyle waited, anticipating the exact moment the raid would start. He glanced up inside his helmet and noted the time was zero two one eight hours Zulu. It was just a little over two hours since the fight of their lives had taken place back at the pass. He saw the faces of Teek and Neel as he spoke to them.

Help get me through this!

Kyle noticed the others all sitting with their fingers nowhere near the triggers of their weapons. Richards had stopped fiddling with his pistol and was in quiet meditation. Underneath his chest armor, Kyle could feel the novel remaining protectively in place over his heart. He flipped through the pierced pages every so often and thought about the arrow Wilcox took to the throat.

My journey could have ended so long ago.

The drop ship engines continued their endless high pitched wail, and the frame vibrated from the sheer power necessary to keep the craft in flight. The occasional dip or sway was countered by the onboard stabilization system, and as a whole the journey was relatively smooth.

Holly called out from the front.

"Here we go!"

The entire troop bay was bathed in red light. Their stomachs floated as the descent began, before any of them were ready for it.

Kyle felt sick for a moment but the restraint straps held him in place. The firm feel of the seat reassured him during the plummet, which was several times faster than a free fall. Richards almost lost control of his carbine and Kyle held more firmly to his own. The over head speakers popped, and a strained voice gave a count down.

"…five…"

Be cool.

"…four…"

Keep focused.

"…three…"

Just follow Richards.

"…two…"

Don't do anything stupid.

"…one…"

Like get yourself killed.

"…mark!"

The drop ship leveled out as the engines screamed, bringing the craft to a sudden stop. The force of the deceleration crushed Kyle into his seat and he strained to hold the carbine between his knees. His stomach tried to flatten his intestines and the blood rushed from his head, which caused a slight gray out. Someone cursed audibly as he lost hold of a carbine. It cascaded on the floor down the row toward Holly who trapped it with a stomp of his foot.

The lights turned a faint green and were subsequently accompanied by a chime. Holly roared into their ears over the helmet radio as he secured the loose weapon.

"GO! GO! GO!"

The troopers pulled their release cords and barreled down the aisles. Kyle was in the middle of his team and followed Richards. In an instant they were outside under the vast open night sky which loomed overhead. The lead troopers began to fire at raiders on the wall as the assault elements advanced. Enemy, dressed in black with flowing robes, were blown from the parapets by the rapid shots of the attack.

The blast of the engines became impossibly loud. The drop ships maintained a steady perch at the top of the walls. Kyle followed Richards as closely as possible with Chen in tow. The group closed in on the stairs as the machineguns positioned at the opposite corners began to fire at the enemy camped outside. Kyle concentrated on sticking to Richards and did not risk looking out over the wall.

With an increased roar, the drop ships gained slight elevation with a flare of their maneuver thrusters which were operating at full burn. The wash from the downdraft, and the fire of the machineguns, were too much for those outside. The enemy routed off into the darkness filled with terror. Their tents were blown into the fires which had been whipped up by the down draft of the drop ships.

As they reached the top of the stairs, Richards shot an armored man off a lower platform nearby. Holly was already at the bottom of the stairs and moved with the speed of a panther. The grab team followed, firing to the left and to the right, cutting down men as they appeared. Kyle shot a large raider dressed only in a loin cloth.

Sorry dude. 'War is hell - but combat's a motherfucker'!

Kyle aimed his carbine to cover the right flank of the team as they ran. Holly continued down a main walkway and fired at anything that moved. The area was a target-rich environment, and the carbines cracked in rapid succession as the troopers advanced through the tent city. The machinegun teams were safely above the line of fire so the assault element ran no risk of hitting them. Kyle was so keyed up that he accidentally shot a stack of clay jugs which exploded in a shower of water.

Calm down! Calm the fuck down!

The group rounded the corner and Kyle could see the large tent that Holly had identified in the briefing. He swung the carbine over his back and pulled the combat pistol from its holster. He took up his assigned position to the right of the entrance and looked to Holly for the signal. As Chen stepped into place, Holly pointed to Kyle who plunged through the door and adjusted his eyes with the help of his low light visor.

Holly moved ahead on the left, stalked low, and covered his zone of fire as he traveled. Kyle mimicked the action on the right; both proceed down a short hallway with Chen and Richards in tow. Ahead, two large armored men who wielded shiny blades burst through a tall curtain. The high caliber pistols leveled themselves on the targets at point blank range, and fired.

Crying out the enemy pitched backward, and landed in disjointed heaps on the ground. Due to the soft texture of the pistol projectiles, the effect was exit wounds nearly the size of a fist and instantaneous death. Kyle kept moving alongside Holly. The two stepped over the bodies in order to reach and tear down the curtain which led to the main chamber of the tent.

Across from them and a few meters away, a single curtain hung down to the floor from the five meter ceiling overhead. Several men, wielding spears, positioned themselves on a large carpet which covered the ground. The grab team went on line and gunned them down without remorse.

Holly moved up to the left of the curtain. Kyle noticed Miller and Regis entering the tent behind them. From the right a man roared out of hiding and Kyle hesitated, unsure if the warrior was the grab target. The sight of the wicked blade heading toward him compelled Kyle to act. The pistol jumped in his hands and the attacker went down like a rag doll. Kyle side stepped over to the curtain opposite Holly, ensuring that Chen and Richards were behind them.

Holly signaled for all to take a knee. With one smooth motion he ripped the curtain down from the ceiling rail that held it in place. As the fabric fell in a rippling motion to the floor, Kyle saw a large raised platform lashed out of timbers and rope. On top was stretched a taut series of hides which held varying types of large pillows and bedding. In the center a thick bodied man along with his attendants froze. He had been trying to fasten on a shirt of scaled mail when the grab team burst in on them.

Without hesitation Holly fired several quick shots. The assistants staggered and fell dead among the bedding in a shower of bone and blood. Kyle was stunned to witness the brutal efficiency with which the man executed his mission. Slowly standing up from his crouch he and numbly stepped toward the edge of the platform.

"Evans! Five o'clock!"

A tremendous blow slammed him from behind and Kyle careened into a platform leg. The smashing force would have knocked him unconscious had he not twisted to take the glancing blow off his helmet. The two hit the ground with a jarring thud and Kyle's pistol flew off into the darkness. Hours of training kicked in as a bellowing command from Holly came through the helmet headphones.

"Fight, Evans, FIGHT!"

Kyle roared and pulled strong, thick fingers from his throat and mouth. He could not lift the man off his back so he began to strike into the darkness with his elbows and swung his head backwards. The elbow blows did not make solid contact but his helmet forcibly struck something causing a satisfying crunch. Now at the advantage, Kyle pulled Neel's blade out from under his arm and sunk it into the upper thigh of the man on his back.

The assailant clamored in pain and shifted his weight. Kyle struggled to maneuver but could not slide out from underneath. As anticipated, the blows began to land against his back. Although his attacker had good position, Kyle's armor effectively absorbed the brunt of the strikes. This contest was nothing like his first encounter in the woods.

Someone crackled in over the head phones.

"Evans, go limp and stay flat!"

Kyle obeyed. Several shots slew his assailant, landing the man across Kyle's lower legs. Scrambling out from under the weight, he recovered his pistol from where it had fallen. Kyle wiped off Neel's blade before sheathing it, and climbed onto the platform. He stepped over the bloody body of one of the attendants to where Holly and Richards had taken hold of the target. Kyle could clearly see the look of shock and indignation on the man's face. To all of their surprise, he lashed out in a rough Universal.

"What hell think you doing?!"

Holly stepped up and struck a blow across the man's jaw that nearly knocked the target unconscious. Richards clasped the hands of the man together while Chen slid on a pair of speed restraints. Kyle stepped past them and cleared the rear of the platform. From there he observed several women who screamed and cowered on the floor. He hesitated, unwilling to murder them in cold blood.

With the help of Miller and Regis, Holly and Richards lifted the target off of the platform. The man staggered slightly on his feet but was easily led out of the tent. Chen took point with Kyle in drag, keeping his attention focused to the rear.

As they emerged into the starlight Kyle switched off the low-light visor to reduce the visual overload. Flames from burning tents and streaking arrows made it difficult to see into the shadows. All around, shouts and firing were heard from the machinegun teams on the wall. Chen was at the bottom of the stairs with his carbine at the ready. Kyle holstered his pistol and swung around his own weapon, keying his helmet microphone.

"This is GRAB 4 to all assault teams, clear the target zone, OVER!"

The demo guys sprinted past as the others responded with an affirmative. Remembering the terrified women behind the platform, Kyle tried to keep his weapon aimed waist high.

It's time to get the hell out of Dodge!

"Let's go people! Let's go!"

He was joined by Chen, and the two fired their carbines on full automatic into the surrounding tents. Several figures spun to the ground as they stepped into the field of fire. Once their weapons emptied Chen led the way up while Richards covered them from above.

While on the wall, a large number of flaming arrows whipped through the air past them with a deadly hiss. Kyle had no idea who the actual target was. It became clear as he witnessed several bounce off the drop ships which made slow circles around the perimeter of the sod wall.

One shaft flashed dangerously close, reminding Kyle of Wilcox's death at the mortars. Angrily he crouched lower and fired a burst in the general direction from which the arrow had come. He was damned if he was going to make it this far only to be felled by some random shot.

From the corners of the sod walls the machineguns tore into the enraged hordes of enemy that had begun to press forward. It was clear that the commanders had regained their wits and were coming to rescue their master. At that very moment the drop ships swung down to the tops of the walls and presented their open waist doors to the waiting troopers.

Kyle made his way past the evil grin on the *King* and briefly regarded the emotionless face of the crew chief. The dark visor of the flight helmet hid most of his features except for the thin line of his mouth. Had he not known better, Kyle would have easily thought him to be a solid stone sculpture.

The assault teams piled into the troop bay and moved down the various rows to find seats. The crew chief was yelling for the machinegun teams and Holly ordered them in from the perimeter. From somewhere outside a flaming arrow had imbedded itself in the inner compartment wall. The waist gunner, who had just been missed, remained focused on the task at hand and blazed away at the dark shapes beyond.

There was a lot of cross chatter on the helmet frequencies along with the constant whine of the engines which could be heard over the rapid cracking of machineguns. The pilots accomplished the impossible and kept the flying behemoths steady and level just off the deck. The machinegun teams appeared at the waist doors, some still firing at the enemy pressing toward them. One was so intent that he had to be pulled bodily inside in order for the doors to close.

Holly strapped in next to the waist gunner and extinguished the burning arrow as the *King* spun out from the extraction point. Kyle and the others grunted and grabbed hold as the drop ship rocketed up and away. The acceleration of the escape crushed the troopers to their respective floor and seat positions while lose captured materials tumbled to the back of the bay.

As the seconds ticked by Kyle had began to gray out from the strain. The pressure finally eased as the *King* made altitude and leveled out to normal flight. The regular lights came on in the bay, and the co-pilot announced that it was safe to move about.

The troopers disentangled themselves as shaky grins appeared. A general banter of relief filled the troop bay. The injured were assessed while others checked and secured their equipment. A small celebration began and even Holly smiled as he slapped troopers on the shoulder in congratulations.

On a more serious note a gunner had taken an arrow to his upper thigh, but a medic was already looking at it with a quiet intensity. Another gave a once-over to the bloody cut on Kyle's jaw, but it proved to be minor in nature. Bleeding head wounds traditionally appeared ten times worse than they really were and Kyle had not even realized he had been cut.

The target was dragged from the floor where he had been tossed and lifted into a chair to which he was bound tightly. He had managed to not utter a sound during the entire ascent and looked around as if trying to make sense of his surroundings. Holly ordered him blindfolded and assigned the prisoner team to keep an eye on him.

The rest of the trip back was uneventful. Troopers talked for a long time and some even showed off their souvenirs to others who had gathered around. Chen displayed a two handed sword still in its ceremonial sheath. Holly picked his way through the crowd, checking on everyone as he passed. He came to sit opposite Kyle and watched the others as they unwound. With a full grin, and without turning, he spoke to Kyle.

"You'll never see anything more truthful than a man happy to be alive after surviving close combat."

Kyle half smiled and nodded his head absently.

"So…I guess we still need to work on your grappling skills."

Kyle instantly felt guilty.

"Yes, Master Sergeant."

Having been taken by complete surprise a second time, Kyle knew he had fought to the best of his ability. The problem was that the raider had him good, and there was nothing Kyle could have done to free himself. If it had not been for the help from Chen, in all likelihood he would have been beaten or even killed. Kyle felt compelled to apologize but kept his mouth shut. Soldiers learned from their mistakes and made every effort to never repeat them.

Holly laughed at him.

"Take it easy Evans. We try to make you guys the best we can in order to keep you and the unit alive. You managed to do that, but there is more that we could be doing to bring you up to speed. The bad guys in this neck of the woods like to stroll up to a soldier and bang on him with a sharp weapon. That's not something you troopers were trained for. We'll just have to start training up to help compensate for the disparity. We just need to hold on until pick-up arrives."

Kyle nodded his head then looked down.

"When do you think they'll come, Master Sergeant?"

Holly thought for a moment.

"Hell if I know. If the *Rosalie* made it back in one piece then it is only a matter of time for them to come looking for us. Regardless, our mission is to hold out and hold on."

Kyle nodded his head as this sunk in.

We may be here for another week or forever.

"The rangers have been performing very well and the commander is more pleased than pissed with what you have accomplished with the natives."

Kyle warmed at this acknowledgement. Holly watched the troopers nearby as they continued to razz each other over who had been scared the most. They had that timeless quality of young men glad to be alive.

"When we get back we're going to have to secure the battlefield around the pass. Once that is done there are going to be some changes in the unit organization. Lieutenant thinks we may be here for a while until someone comes for us. In the meantime we are to disperse and establish as strong a presence as we can. This will help us connect with the locals for manpower and support, and make it harder for someone to kill us all from orbit."

Holly looked over to Kyle, who thought about dying from an orbital bombardment.

"That means we have to get you polished up and perfect some of your war fighting skills. We want to assign you and some of the others as platoon leaders for additional auxiliary units."

Kyle looked at him in surprise as Holly continued.

"We are going to establish strongholds in the various regions surrounding the central mountain compound. Each area will have a unit led by troopers that will occupy key terrain and provide local security. This will allow us a safe zone in which to rest, train, and prepare for future operations. The current plan is to get the force up to regimental strength."

Kyle contemplated the size of a regiment - which meant three platoons to a company, three companies to a battalion, and three battalions to make up the whole. It would be quite an undertaking. Kyle thought about Taulk and the rest of his squad.

"What about my rangers, Master Sergeant?"

Holly shrugged his shoulders.

"There is still a need for local security so the natives will be deployed to protect our current ground assets. Based on the recommendations of the squad leaders, individual natives will be tapped to step into leadership roles and assume command of their units."

If I had to put my life in the hands of a ranger it would be Taulk.

Kyle took all of this in.

"Roger that, Master Sergeant. It seems we'll have our hands full for a while."

Holly nodded his head as if only to himself. Kyle looked over to where the target sat blindfolded and asked,

"What's going to happen to him?"

Holly turned and looked at the man. The target was in his mid forties and a little under average height. His head was already balding and his stomach showed the effects of too much eating without enough exercise. Regardless of how he had earned his position he was, nonetheless, a sad looking specimen.

"Him we're going to toss into an underground holding cell for a few days. Since we know he speaks Universal we should be able to get through to him with little 'encouragement'. We need to see if that army of his will disperse after it lost its head – along with experiencing the sheer shock of being attacked in two different places by dragons and the baddest mothers to come out of the sky."

Kyle grinned at this.

"Do you think he is The One?"

Holly stared at the man for a while and then shook his head.

"I don't think so. Even though he can speak it, his Universal is clearly a second language. I think this One is hidden away in some stronghold that will be a hell of a lot harder to crack than that circus tent we just raided. I'm sure this fellow will have some interesting stories to tell us though."

With that, the senior man got up and moved toward the front of the bay. Kyle sat and listened to the dull roar of the engines as most of the others drifted off to sleep. As his own eyes closed, visions of screaming men with blades and fire waged fierce battle in his exhausted mind. They tore at each other, and sometimes lashed out at him, to which his body could only flinch in reply.

Kyle watched the flamethrower blasting the mass of enemy pressing up the slope at the pass. Teek was stretched out on the ground in front of the village barricade with his eyes staring. Kyle tried to straighten the tunic of the dead man but the corpse grabbed him by the throat and began to choke him. The maggot covered face that looked at him now was that of the slain hunter in the woods.

Kyle awoke with a start and finding himself still strapped to the troop seat. He released the upper most clip of his body armor to help rid himself of the death grip sensation to his throat. Looking around, he saw the other sleeping troopers passed out in various contorted poses. The drop ship began to descend and a moment later the engines flared landing with a gentle bump. Sergeants prodded the weary troopers into action; the mass of spent men finding the energy to move. As they offloaded the drop ship Kyle watched the sun rise in the eastern sky and found himself too exhausted to care much about anything.

* * *

CHAPTER X

The Battle of Mountain Pass took several days to clean up. Tens of thousands of dead raiders and slain dogs were dragged far out into the steppe and left there to rot. There was no manpower available to dig the mass grave needed for so many to be buried. A good number of prisoners were rounded up and stripped of their possessions, only to be put to work dragging off their less fortunate comrades and beasts.

The defeated were marked with a large one-inch bolt head which was dipped in a mild acid. The octagon shape left an obvious scar unlike anything the natives had ever seen before. All bearers of this 'mark of the dragon' were warned that if encountered in this part of the steppe again their lives would be forfeit. They were then given enough hard tack for a few days travel and ordered to return from whence they came.

Thus spared, the prisoners were released with their wounded companions to a fate unknown in the tall steppe grass. Most left without a second look, and those who lingered did not remain for long.

Captured enemy leaders were held in a detention camp later to be interrogated by the intelligence section. In time, a decision would be made as to whether they would be released or not. The target quickly changed his uncooperative mood once he saw the waste laid to the corps of cavalry he had sent against the village. The ego-driven native warmed readily to the superior treatment he received from his interrogators, and soon shared as much information as he knew.

Most of the time he talked of a powerful master whose rule spread across the steppe to the northeast. As best intelligence could determine, the man arrived during the Night of Fire more than a decade ago, and was hailed by the tribes as the son of a dark god. The One made the most out of being a Child of the Darkness, and had apparently used his newly found influence to its fullest advantage.

In the mean time the village folk seized all of the booty to be had from the battle field and stockpiled the weapons and armor in a livery stable near the main square. This equipment would be cleaned, inventoried, and later used to equip the new infantry units that would soon patrol the border with the steppe. The remainder of the loot would be divided amongst the villagers as reward for their support, with additional compensation being given to those who had lost family members during the fight.

The dogs that refused to submit to handlers, or were too badly wounded, were destroyed. The rest were herded into large holding pens just inside the edge of the valley located behind the village. Here the animals were separated and vetted as cavalry mounts. The rangers that knew how to ride were issued an animal and organized into patrols. These cavalry detachments were then sent out to monitor the dispersal of the defeated and to serve as an early warning against other threats. The remaining animals were left to breakers who immediately started training the beasts for useful service.

With the new regiment created Lieutenant Taylor assumed the honorary rank of Colonel. He released the drop ships back to their mountain dwelling in order for them to conduct light maintenance. By sending the ships away he would also preserve their shock effect on the populace and allow the mystique of the dragons to continue. He well recalled the terror the craft had caused to the enemy during the air assault raid. Stranded on a foreign world, the Colonel would take any advantage he was offered.

The constant demand placed upon the ships in recent months began to take its toll, especially in the operating environment of the planet. Without maintenance facilities like those on the *Rosalie,* the behemoths could not be thoroughly serviced. In addition, the Fleet commander wanted to eliminate every unnecessary minute in the air.

There was a brief discussion about investigating the mysterious Darkness that moved above them. The Colonel decided that it was not a risk the regiment could afford to take at that time. Discovering what role the black object might play in the big scheme of things would have to wait. Taylor felt that he could not afford to split his force, especially by sending personnel off the planet. The main goal of the regiment was to recruit more locals into the ranks and firmly establish itself in the region. Fortunately for him the Flight leader agreed.

The flight crews were stationed with their ships deep in the mountain valley where the original compound was established all those months ago. Security consisted of a fire team composed entirely of troopers who guarded the main entrance to the cavern. The relief and pick-up by Fleet was still an unknown variable. The drop ships would continue taking turns, checking on a signal buoy left in high orbit. It was meant to attract the attention of any friendly vessel or probe that might Fold into the system. These hops were also used to collect better topographical data and provide the crews an opportunity to conduct aerial reconnaissance while making the trip.

It was several weeks later when disaster struck.

During one of the hops an emergency transmission was received from the *King*. The pilot called a mayday to any station and announced that the ship was going down. The call was brief, hectic, and one way. Attempts to contact the drop ship went unanswered. The *Ace* scrambled and the crew arrived in the general area within twenty minutes of dispatch. The pilot searched the crisscross mountain gullies and valleys but found no trace of the *King* from the air. A passive scan of high orbit indicated no contact. Rumor quickly circulated that the incident had something to do with the Darkness.

Speculation soon ran rampant as to exactly what had happened to the *King*. The data scans provided by the *Ace* were carefully scrutinized a second time in order to eliminate the possibility of having missed any trace of enemy activity - to no avail. Others, still, suggested the lack of sufficient overhaul maintenance appeared to be the main culprit. After much deliberation, and elimination of theories derived from the facts at hand, it was finally decided that maintenance, indeed, was the most likely suspect. With this chilling conclusion the

Colonel took no further risks and requested that the *Ace* and *Joker* be grounded for the unforeseeable future. The new Flight leader consented and the remaining crews stood down.

Taylor immediately ordered a search and recovery mission to scour the area. The 3rd Battalion received the mission and word passed down to the companies that they had been selected. India Company, also known as Franklin's Minions, was the unit to which Kyle found himself reassigned as a platoon leader. With his new title he was also given the responsibility of training thirty new native recruits and getting them disciplined, more or less, like troopers.

* * *

Kyle pulled himself into the saddle of his mount and tried to keep his eyes open. He had been running non-stop to ensure that all essential equipment and provisions were packed, and that every last man in the platoon was ready for action. Breaking in his new squad leaders was not easy but they seemed eager and willing to learn. Word of his prior service with the rangers, and a well timed visit from Taulk, had apparently preceded his arrival to the platoon. The result was minimal hassle and maximum effort on the part of his new charges.

Reaching down, Kyle scratched his dog behind its ears. He decided to name the animal Gorbash after a fictional dragon of his youth. The creature raised its massive head slightly and panted in the morning air. Kyle had grown to trust the beast which was paired to him by the native breakers who had evaluated both of their personalities. Even though the basic trust was there, the realization that it took just one wrong move by the five hundred pound animal to ruin his day was never far off. Kyle often wondered what treatment the animal had experienced at the hands of his previous owners. Many of the dogs had numerous scars from prior rough handling.

I'll bet being a Horde mount was no picnic.

Up ahead he saw Rey pass back the hand signal in preparation for mounting. Kyle's old squad leader had been assigned a platoon under Franklin as well. Kyle waved back an acknowledgement and ordered his squad leaders to get the platoon ready. As they scattered in a hubbub of hasty orders, spoken in native tongue, Kyle turned to the small gathering of troopers at his side. Richards was talking and had the attention of the others.

"…So if you think about it, 'draco' means 'dragon', and 'dracula' means 'son of the dragon'. We could just call ourselves something cool like that instead."

The others stared at Richards for a moment in mute disbelief. Buster shook his head with indignation and muttered under his breath,

"Dracula? Richards, you are one freaky dude. There is no way I'm naming myself after a blood sucking vampire."

The others all grinned and chuckled. Richards looked up at Kyle as if appealing to a higher power. Kyle just shrugged his shoulders.

"Sorry man, I'm not feeling it."

Dejected, Richards seemed to retire into deeper thought. The others gathered around to tap fists with Kyle before departing.

"Hang in there man."

"Take it easy 'LT'."

"Remember to take a buddy with you to the latrine."

Kyle threw Buster a look as the trooper feigned surprise at the reaction to his advice. The others laughed and moved back to make way for Gorbash as the animal side-stepped under the weight of his rider. Up ahead Rey called out to his own platoon.

"Prepare to mount!"

Kyle echoed the command to his own squad leaders who were watching and waiting. They passed the order to their squad members, who had coaxed their dogs into a disorderly column of twos. The entire battalion had only had a few short weeks to become familiar with their mounts and it showed. Kyle noted that every last pair of eyes in the platoon was on him, waiting for the next order.

Good, very good. I think these guys are going to work out.

"Mount!"

The men stepped up into their saddles and quickly controlled their shifting dogs. Rey stood high in his stirrups, and with one arm raised, relayed the preparatory command.

"For-ward!'

Kyle did the same. He risked a quick survey of the troopers who watched on with empty expressions and reserved spirits.

I may never see any of them ever again.

In unison with Rey he dropped his arm and gave the order.

"March!"

The column lurched into motion. The others gathered nearby burst into a chant of friendly cat calls, assorted hoots, and whistles. Kyle tried to remember the details of their faces as his buddies all saluted in unison. Returning the gesture, he suddenly felt very alone and unwilling to leave them behind. Although he knew Rey, Kyle was only vaguely familiar with his new captain and had but a passing familiarity with the executive officer. The other platoon leader was just recently assigned and still completely unknown to him.

I don't even know what the guy looks like!

As the column proceeded out of the village toward the west, Kyle thought about the journey that had brought him to where he was today. He thought of Neel and Teek, as well as the other troopers he had known for the long months when they had struggled together to survive. Worse, still, was the faint recollection of his birth family and friends on planets far away, which seemed more imagined than real.

Reaching up with his hand Kyle touched the hilt of Neel's dagger and thought of the rangers guarding the approach from the steppe. Most of his old squad had been promoted to head troops of their own. Holly, tapped to serve as the Regimental Sergeant Major, had passed along Kyle's recommendation for the selection of Taulk to lead an infantry company of his own. The native was more of a brother now, and it felt odd leaving the ranger to his own fate.

As the morning sun began to climb into the eastern sky behind them, Kyle adjusted his carbine across his chest. Having tried several different sling configurations he found this was the best for keeping the weapon out of the way but readily accessible. Thus positioned, he could control Gorbash and still fire effectively with just one hand. Looking down Kyle checked the quick release straps which held several light axes to his riding saddle.

When 24th century fails you, just switch to the 9th century for backup!

Kyle smiled to himself, amused by the notion that he enlisted as a trooper in a military with advanced technology that was now reduced to dependence on archaic hand weapons. Transportation used to be facilitated by gigantic carriers that could whisk entire divisions across the vastness of space in the blink of an eye. Now the most reliable mode of transportation was a huge oversized canine. Kyle was thankful for small favors though, as he retained use of the combat armor and helmet features which still functioned. The regiment would need every edge over the other hostiles just to survive.

As the column advanced, the village of Mountain Pass disappeared behind them with only the smoke of breakfast fires marking its location. The remainder of the morning was a boring routine of swaying in the saddle with only an occasional stop to water the dogs in the river or to give them some rest.

Traveling on Gorbash was a relatively quiet experience and the journey was a wonderful introduction to the valley they had bypassed in the airlift. The breeze was sweet and gentle with large conifer trees swaying as if dancing in their sleep. Ahead the spectacular mountain ridges swept up from either side and climbed high to the horizon, reaching for the tops of several different peaks capped with white snow.

Major Medina commanded the battalion and urged the men ever forward. As the column continued west, small groups of villagers appeared, heading in the opposite direction toward their homes. Most of them were older except for the women who had their children in tow.

These travelers kept their distance while noting the dark green banners with the emblem of a golden pine tree; each denoting the three ranger companies in the battalion. The children all smiled and waved as several of the rangers grinned and returned the greeting. Kyle smiled as a small girl rushed forward toward the riders, ignoring the harsh chastisement of an older woman.

The little one stopped short and looked up into his tired eyes dissociated from the effects of battle. She broke into a huge grin and began giggling. Turning in a pirouette, she shrieked playfully, running back to the arms of her ward, who shook a warning finger, and gave her a single small spank.

The rangers ate as they rode. After a while the constant jarring in the saddle started to transfer to their backs and necks. The sun began to descend in front of them and the darkness of the evening crawled out of hiding from the valley floor. Slowly the battalion circled into a defensive coil and pickets were stationed to give early warning of an enemy approach. After checking on his platoon, Kyle covered himself with a rough riding blanket and fell asleep against the thick fur coat of Gorbash.

The battalion continued to press west into the mountains for the next several days. Medina kept the column moving at a fast clip, stopping only long enough to rest and feed the mounts. Despite the quick pace, Kyle was frustrated. He wished there was a faster way for the unit to move in hopes of locating the downed drop ship and crew.

Then again, maybe this is purely a recovery effort by now.

The thought left an unpleasant feeling in his gut. The men, for the most part, took turns sleeping in their saddles, having tied themselves in to prevent falling. The defensive coil was the same each night. The only perceivable difference was the continued cooling of the air as the column penetrated farther into the mountains.

On the evening of the fifth day Rey signaled for his platoon to halt and Kyle echoed the command to his own men. Soon a runner appeared and summoned the officers to the front of the column. As Kyle spurred Gorbash forward he could make out the high stone wall of a small town ahead.

The evening torches were being lit as he watched, and two large braziers burned brightly on either side of an entrance to a timber gate house. Franklin waited for Kyle and Rey to halt near him before turning and nodding to Medina. Although the battalion commander addressed the captains, the lieutenants could also clearly hear what was said.

"The lead scout says these people are reasonably friendly. I want you to ensure that your sergeants keep the men on a tight leash. They now represent the regiment and will be held to the highest standards of behavior and obedience. I am going to parley with our good friend over there guarding the main gate, and see if we can't sleep inside the walls this evening instead of out in the cold. Wait here."

With that, Medina accompanied by an adept native scout, turned his dog toward the entrance. As the two entered the ring of firelight, a challenge came from the gate house wall above them. The riders halted momentarily before the scout nudged his dog a step closer. Kyle watched as the native man gestured a greeting and began speaking in a harsh guttural language.

After a short discourse the native turned in his saddle to Medina. Kyle could just make out what was said.

"He say he not open gate until morrow."

Medina looked from the lead scout to the face of the man lit by the torch light. Kyle could see the guard appraise the column of armored rangers as they stretched out into the darkness. Medina turned back to the lead scout with further instructions.

"Ask him if there is an officer in charge that I may speak with."

The scout translated accordingly. The man from the wall responded with a brief reply and seemed to ask a question in response. The scout turned back in his saddle.

"He say that you must be a person of power, for him risk beating by officer."

Medina turned to Franklin with a look of bemusement, to which the captain could only shrug his shoulders. Medina turned back to the lead scout who watched the officers with a sort of bored curiosity.

"Ask him if he has heard of the great battle at the mountain pass near the steppe five days east of here."

The lead scout turned back to the man, who was most likely the sergeant of the guard, and translated the question. The man on the wall replied with a single tilting of his head to the right. The lead scout turned back to Medina who gestured that he understood.

"Tell this man that I am part of that mighty army, as are these men behind me, which met the Horde of The One and destroyed it in battle."

The lead scout hesitated for a moment, trying to figure how best to translate the declaration to the waiting man on the wall. With grand pronouncement, and a wide wave of his arm to Kyle and the others, the lead scout delivered what could only be described as a noble attempt.

The man on the wall seemed to take this all in for a moment or two. He spoke a few words, and then disappeared from view. The lead scout turned back to Medina.

"Sir, man say wait."

Medina sighed with a slight irritation.

"I already appear to be doing that."

A call went up from inside the wall and several faces peered through the various firing slits around the gate house. Spears materialized high in the night sky betraying the position of their owners who also looked down questioningly on the strange riders and their dogs. Several more minutes passed and then another series of orders were heard, followed soon thereafter by the opening of a smaller door within the larger gate. A man wearing a white tabard over shiny chain armor stepped through. He had no helmet and sported an ornate mace which swung freely from his left hip.

This warrior approached to within yards of Medina before coming to a halt. Several men and the sergeant accompanied him but remained a respectful distance behind. The man looked up at Medina. He had fierce eyes and jet black hair with a well trimmed beard. He seemed well kempt but showed signs of rough frontier living.

"This is Robier. He is Law for town."

The Law betrayed his surprise as the scout spoke. Kyle realized that the man could understand Universal. Medina appeared to realize this as well, and to the Law inquired,

"You can understand what we are saying?"

The man recovered his composure before answering the question. When he spoke, his voice was firm and strong.

"I understand perfectly. I am just surprised to hear it spoken so well by complete strangers."

Kyle was shocked, as the Law was much more fluent in Universal than the battalion's own rangers. With a slight motion of his head, the major sent the scout back to the column and looked at the Law. It seemed the man had questions of his own.

"How is it that you speak the tongue of the Sky? It is a skill taught only to a few and it is rare for you to be as fluent as you are."

The question had a hint of suspicion to it which Kyle could understand. The only other person who spoke Universal was locked up back at Mountain Pass. Medina sat back in his saddle and let out a long sigh.

"Well, to be perfectly honest, I have been speaking it my whole life. Of course there are a few nuns who would beg to differ."

The Law did not seem to understand the jest. He instead looked at Franklin and the other officers who were gathered around.

"They all know the tongue of the Sky as well?"

Medina nodded absently, correcting himself by tilting his head to the right in the native fashion.

"All of my officers are fluent in what we call Universal. In fact, most of our sergeants speak it well enough to hold a conversation. A good portion of the men in the battalion can understand orders when spoken."

The Law seemed to digest this. Kyle sensed that the man was searching for something by the line of his questioning; Medina did not seem to realize it. The Law crossed his arms.

"You say you fought in the large battle near the steppe?"

Medina tilted his head to the right in reply.

"It is said then that you have powerful weapons at your disposal."

Medina hesitated, but once again tilted his head to the right. The Law now spoke as a man who had placed his cards on the table.

"Do you come from Peace?"

Medina cast a questioning glance. He looked briefly at the others to be sure that he had heard the Law correctly.

"Peace? I am sorry, but I do not understand what you mean. We are not here to harm you if that is your concern."

The Law did not appear to entirely understand Medina. After apparently convincing himself of some unknown fact he spoke again.

"Peace is the mountain domain of a people rumored to be Children of the Darkness."

The man turned and pointed to the north. Kyle glanced up and could make out the peaks of the mountains as dark cuts against a star filled sky. The Law continued,

"They were first discovered many years ago not long after the Night of Fire. Bright flashes and streaks of light heralded their arrival for several nights in a row. They brought with them great power which they used to destroy anyone sent against them. It was they who taught a survivor the tongue of Sky so that we would understand that they wished only to be left alone in Peace."

Medina tilted his head to the left in denial. The Law seemed to try and read Medina's expression before he spoke again.

"It is said that you are the Sons of Dragons who fight for you."

For a moment the question seemed to catch Medina off guard but he thought and tilted his head to the right again.

"Yes, it is true that we have help from that which you call dragons."

Kyle watched the face of the stranger as the man listened. The Law asked in a cool, calm voice:

"Have you come for the fallen dragon then?"

Medina tensed.

"Yes. Do you know where it is?"

The Law slowly pointed back toward the mountain.

"Several nights journey away and well within the kingdom of Peace."

Kyle sat back in his saddle.

Great! Juuust great….

Medina seemed to think this over. After a moment the Law turned to his sergeant and uttered a few brief instructions. The subordinate hurried the others back toward the gate with a curt bark and wave of the arm. There appeared to be a change of heart but the Law did not move. Instead, he turned and spoke to Medina,

"How many men will you need accommodations for?"

Medina studied the stranger briefly.

"Around two hundred troopers and their mounts."

The Law accepted this and pointed toward the torch lit wall. The massive wooden gate swung inward and the sergeant of the guard appeared with several more men who lined up along each side of the road. All wore helmets, some loosely affixed, and carried a rough pole slightly taller with a glistening spear tip.

"The sergeant will lead you to a field we have located inside the wall. Your men can rest and set up camp there. We will see what supply requests we can satisfy in the morning. You and your officers are our guests - if you would accept our courtesy. Please follow me."

The Law strode off toward the entrance and Medina turned to his captains to get their initial impressions. Franklin simply shrugged his shoulders and looked to the others, who did the same. With no protests offered, Medina turned and urged his dog toward the gateway. Franklin and the other captains turned to their gathered officers and rode back to join their individual commands. Rey gave Kyle a reassuring grin and nodded as the two separated to rejoin their men.

After a brief lull the column jostled into motion and the troopers quietly filed in through the archway. As Kyle entered the town he was somewhat startled to see the Law on a flight of stone steps, flanked by two bright torches. The man seemed to wait for each of the troopers, easily distinguished by his combat armor, as he rode by.

"Welcome, Sons of Dragons."

Kyle was unsure of what to do, but did not want to be rude, and slightly bowed his head to acknowledge the greeting. Gorbash continued to pad forward, and led the platoon along a rough stone street which twisted through a large square. As he looked back at his riders, Kyle watched as the large wooden gates slowly swung shut behind them.

No turning back now.

He realigned his position to the front as he led his rangers out of the torch lit area and into the cool darkness of the enclosed field beyond. He looked up to the night sky and absently searched for the Darkness, though he knew it was not yet above the horizon. His thoughts turned to the morning, when they would go out looking for the *King* and in search of Peace.

* * *

THE BEGINNING